Disengaged

VALERIE LANDRUM

Year of the Book

135 Glen Avenue

Glen Rock, PA 17327

ISBN 13: 978-1-942430-59-9

ISBN 10: 1-942430-59-0

To my parents, Clarence and Elizabeth Landrum.

Acknowledgments

There are so many people that made this project come to fruition.

My fellow members of the SSA Six: Alice, Deena, Karen, Norma and Renee, who encouraged me despite my defiant nature.

The ones who read this as a very rough draft: Gina, Chrissy, Cynthia, Deborah, and Renita.

Demi, editor extraordinaire, who turned a run-on story into a book!

Chapter 1

I wondered how I would be able to walk past him unnoticed. It had been four years since we last saw each other. Would he even recognize me? Who was I kidding? I certainly recognized him. Nicholas looked great. I needed to look away before he noticed me staring.

"Alex, just go up to him. You know you want to," I heard my sister say.

"Stephanie, I am engaged. Nicholas doesn't mean anything to me anymore," I said, hoping I sounded more confident than I felt.

My sister was skeptical, "If that was true, you wouldn't be scared to talk to him. Now just go and wiggle your little black ass in front of the man and see what he does about it."

There was also the Patricia factor, my holier-than-thou, future sister-in-law, who would be joining us for lunch at any moment. She would love to tell my fiancé Keith that she saw me with another man, even if it was innocent.

Necessity ended up ruling the day. I had to use the ladies room, which put me near him. He was talking to another man at the bar, so I felt I might make it by him unnoticed. I took three steps around before the click of my low-heeled pumps must've drawn his attention. He stood and reached out for my arm. "Hi Alex, I hope you weren't trying to avoid me."

A familiar tingle ran up my arm, despite the long sleeves of my sweater.

"Of course not," I lied. "How are you, Nicholas?" He pulled me into a hug. He still smelled good, too.

"I'm great now. How are you?" he whispered in my ear.

"Wonderful, I'm engaged." I may have said that too quickly.

I pulled back from those broad shoulders, which were hidden under a more expensive suit jacket than he used to wear.

Did his eyes lose a little luster when he heard I was engaged?

"Lucky man," he said softly.

"And I am a lucky woman. Take care, Nicholas," I said and walked away.

When I sat back down, Stephanie had to comment. "He watched you walk all the way back to your seat. Did you give him your phone number?"

"I am engaged to be married. That means I no longer give my number to men."

"You are not married yet, besides Nicholas is a lot more than just a man. If things had happened differently, you wouldn't be with Keith."

I was about to school my sister when Patricia showed up and I had to table the conversation.

"Hello ladies, sorry I'm late," Patricia said as she sat down. "I hope I didn't miss anything."

I stared my sister into silence. Lunch continued uneventfully. I was relieved to see that when we were ready to leave, Nicholas had apparently already gone.

Stephanie followed me to my car and whispered, "Have a great evening," before sprinting over to her parking space.

I went back to work, but my mind kept wandering. Why was he affecting me like this? Nicholas was my past. Keith is my present and future. I could not afford to be caught up in the mess all over again.

When I first met Nicholas, I was 19 and just starting my sophomore year in college. My friend Tamika had dragged me to a frat party. I was practically hugging a wall, when he walked over to me. I was nervous, this man wanted to talk to me, when there were girls dressed in half the clothes I wore, eyeing him all night.

"I'm Nicholas," he said extending his hand.

"I'm Alexandra," I said softly, taking in the view. Nicholas was tall. I had to tilt my head a little to see his eyes. Nicholas was caramel brown. Did I mention I loved caramel? He smiled like he had it all under control.

I found out there was some substance to the man as well. He was at the top of his class, finishing up his BS/MBA in finance. Nicholas planned to be a CEO by age 30. He was also single and childless.

The romance was amazing. Nicholas made everything seem perfect. For the first time, I was really enjoying life. I was even defying my parents, who did not like Nicholas at all. They thought he was just using me. I loved him and I know he loved me. I had never had a real relationship before so maybe my judgment was colored, but I was happy.

I always thought I'd remain a virgin until marriage, but I let Nicholas have my virginity, with no regrets. When I found out I was pregnant with his baby, I was not nearly as scared as I thought I would be.

Unfortunately, my happiness was soon shattered.

I took a long soothing bubble bath when I got home to clear my head and prepare for my evening with Keith. I debated about what to wear. We did not have any plans to go out, but I still wanted to look nice, but not too nice. My fiancé is newly saved so according to him, we can't have sex again until our wedding night. I must be careful not to tempt him.

It's going to be a long five months.

Chapter 2

I was just taking dinner out of the oven when the doorbell rang. Keith had arrived with flowers.

"Thank you," I said kissing him. "You are so sweet."

"You're welcome." Keith took off his coat and hung it neatly in my hall closet.

He is not as tall as Nicholas, but he's the same shade of caramel. Keith is such a sweet man, loyal to me and his family. He would never be as reckless as Nicholas. He is calm and rational. I love him, and from this point on, I swear I'll stop comparing him to Nicholas.

As we ate the lovely roast and vegetables I made, we talked about our day. A certain subject, of course, was never mentioned. Keith knew about Nicholas, and I knew about his significant relationships. But I was never going to see Nicholas again, so there was no point in bringing up today's chance meeting.

"I had lunch today with Patricia and Stephanie to discuss the wedding."

"Umm. How did that go?" Keith asked, expecting the worst.

"It went fine. The two are coming to terms with one another."

"I was just asking," he said, cutting another perfectly sized bite of roast. "You know your sister can be a little..."

I raised my eyebrows at that comment. "My sister? What about yours? Patricia can be a little overbearing. She thinks she has to have the final say on everything. You would think this was her wedding."

"She just wants us to have a beautiful Christian wedding."

"And what, my little sister is the Anti-Christ?"

Keith calmly put down his fork. "I didn't say that. Our sisters just see things differently. Can we just leave it at that?"

The last thing I wanted to do was fight with my man. We could be doing other things, within limits. We settled on the couch to watch a movie. I snuggled up against Keith, nuzzling his neck. He liked that. We were making out before too long. Then he pulled back.

"We better stop."

"Are you sure?" I asked, reaching for his top button.

Immediately, he sat up. "We should call it a night."

"Already? It's not even 8:30. Keith, aren't you carrying this virtuous thing a little too far?"

"Believe me. You'll thank me for this once we're married."

And he left. Did I mention it was going to be a long five months?

I was just changing from my nice demure buttoned up blouse and long skirt into my looney tunes nightshirt when the phone rang. I checked the name without thinking. *It was him.* My breath caught in my throat. I almost didn't pick up. And I probably should have stayed with that first instinct.

"Hello."

"Hi, Alex. Are you surprised to hear from me?"

"I am. How did you get my number?"

"I cannot reveal my sources."

"I bet I could guess."

"Don't be mad. Is your boyfriend around?"

"No, he just left," I said and immediately regretted it.

"How could he leave you alone all night? The brother has a lot to learn."

"Is that why you called, to disparage my fiancé?"

"Not at all, I called to talk to you. I haven't stopped thinking about you since I saw you today. It brought back a flood of memories, good memories."

"And bad."

There was a long silence before Nicholas spoke again. Gone was the usual confidence. "I'm sorry. I never meant for it to happen. If I could change it, I would. I loved you and our baby."

"Nicholas, I know that. Don't blame yourself. Things happen for a reason. It wasn't meant for us to be parents back then. I forgave you a long time ago."

"Thank you. I think I needed to hear you say that. I wouldn't want to live the rest of my life with you hating me."

"I never hated you. What went on in our relationship was always consensual. When you started doing destructive things to yourself, I could have left, but I thought my love could change you."

"I stopped. I'm completely clean now. Not one ounce since the accident."

I wanted to cry. Nicholas was finally clean. The drugs that were the other woman in our relationship, the drugs that probably led him to fall asleep that night and crash the car, killing our unborn child, were no longer a part of his life.

"Good, I always knew you were too smart to think coke would enhance your career."

"It cost me a lot more than a career."

My breath caught in my throat. *Why couldn't he have realized that years ago?* "From what I saw today, you are still quite a catch. I can't believe there isn't some woman trying to attach herself to you."

"What am I supposed to do? There isn't anybody who compares to you, Alex."

"Thank you, but I'm sure there is somebody out there for you." I'm thinking why is he doing this to me? I am about to melt. Keith, why did you have to go home so early?

"Can we have dinner some night?"

"I'm engaged, I cannot date other men."

"It doesn't have to be a date. Just two friends having dinner."

If I shut him down once and for all, he'll stop calling me and I can stop having flashbacks. I'm having enough trouble with this celibacy stuff anyway. Just say no, just say no.

"What about lunch?" I heard myself say, and then I didn't retract it. I waited for his reply.

"Sure, when and where?"

I couldn't sleep that night. I had let myself be manipulated into going out with Nicholas. Why did I do that? Well I could always not show up. I could use my lunch hour to kill my sister for giving Nicholas my phone number.

Chapter 3

If I had any sense, I would have called my mother and told her about my plans to see Nicholas. She would have gladly locked me in her basement until the feeling wore off. Of course, I did not tell her my plans. I proceeded to get dressed for work. I'd like to think I didn't take any extra care in my outfit or makeup on this day. Nor did I spend extra time in the mirror assessing my flaws and attributes. I looked good in my navy dress that fit very well and stopped an inch or so before my knees and even more so when I sat down. I let my hair fall around my shoulders today instead of putting it in a clip. I wore some nice heels to boost my height a few inches.

As I parked, I saw him step out of a black BMW and walk toward the restaurant. I had the chance to drive away and keep things from going too far. Was I really doing this?

He stood as I approached the table. "You look beautiful."

"Thank you," I dared not verbalize my thoughts of him.

"Thank you for joining me. I wasn't sure if I had permanently burned that bridge."

"I think you know that couldn't happen. Once upon a time, you were my everything."

"And you mine. So is this engagement thing set in stone? Do you have a wedding date?"

"Yes, Keith and I are getting married July 27th."

"So I have five months to convince you you're making a mistake," Nicholas said taking my hand.

I gently removed my hand from his. "Nicholas, I know I'm not making a mistake. Keith and I are in love. We want the same things in life. He is a wonderful Christian man."

"I'm sure that pleases your mother. She called me a heathen so many times; I was beginning to think it was my real name."

"Well, my mother does have her opinion on things."

"I am serious about changing your mind," he said looking into my eyes.

"Nicholas, you can't change my mind. You just saw me yesterday for the first time in four years. You don't know anything about me anymore. I don't know you either. It's over for us."

"So why did you come?"

I took a deep breath. Why did I come? Wasn't I curious? If there was nothing left, why would I care? I didn't have an answer.

"Maybe I just wanted to tell you that in person."

Neither one of us believed that. "Alex, one of your many attributes is your inability to lie worth a damn."

I thought maybe if we talked about things other than our relationship, I might feel less guilty. Nicholas had not made CEO, however he was training for an executive management position. He was still single of course, and childless. His sister Danielle had just graduated from college last summer. His parents were still running their store in East Baltimore.

"Alex, I want to see you again. Is dinner too soon?"

I got back to work just in time to take Keith's call on my desk phone. As we talked, my cell was ringing and it was Nicholas. I let it go to voicemail.

"Are you listening to me?" Keith said with irritation in his voice.

"Yes, I am listening. You want us to have dinner at your parents' house on Sunday."

"Right."

"So are you coming over tonight?" I asked not sure whether I wanted him to or not.

"I was thinking that after last night, we probably need to limit our alone time from now until the wedding."

"So what does that mean? We can only talk on the phone, exchange email and texts or be chaperoned?"

"Alex, it's not as bad as all that. You'll be thanking me for my discipline when we're married."

"That's what you keep saying. I hope you're right. I gotta go. Love you."

I spent the rest of the day telling myself, I had a good Christian man and I should be grateful for him. I have gone longer than five months without having sex before. I love Keith. I want to be his wife. I will do what I must for us to have a happy and Christian-centered marriage.

I had hoped Keith and I could have some weekend time together. We did go to a movie Friday night, but afterwards, he dropped me off at home. I resigned myself to a lonely night in bed with only a book to keep me company.

It wasn't long before my phone rang. It wasn't Keith.

"What is wrong with that guy? He leaves you all alone on a Friday night. I can come over and keep you company."

"No, you cannot."

"There's always tomorrow."

"Look, Nicholas, this is not a good idea. I'm glad you're doing well. I'm doing well. Let's leave it at that."

"Why? Because you have a boyfriend? It seems to me, he's not giving you the attention you deserve."

"It's not your concern, Nicholas," I said, though he'd nailed it perfectly. "I repeat, I'm doing just fine. Goodnight."

Chapter 4

I have no idea why I thought it would be that easy to get rid of Nicholas. I slept uneasily for a long time. As soon as I was deeply into it, I woke to someone knocking on my door.

It couldn't be him.

It was him.

"Hold on," I said through the door and ran back to my bedroom to take off my scarf and cover my nightshirt with a robe.

I opened the door for him. He strode in like he lived there and swept me up in his arms for a hug and kiss that I nearly broke my neck to keep from receiving on the lips.

"Why are you here?" I asked when my feet touched the ground again.

"What's wrong with having breakfast with a beautiful woman?"

"What if I say no?"

"Then I'll wait for lunch."

I guess I walked right into that one. "Oh Lord, Nicholas, what am I supposed to do with you?"

The smile answered the question before he spoke. "First, get dressed so we can go eat, then we'll figure out the rest."

I should have thrown him out. I should have called Keith or my Mom. I should have done anything other than what I did, which was to shower, get dressed and go to breakfast with him. Nicholas was so confident, it bordered on arrogance. Just because he was tall, handsome, smart and successful didn't make him a woman's dream.

Yes it did. At least he used to be my dream.

Nicholas was a perfect gentleman, helping me with my coat, holding the car door for me, and holding my chair at the restaurant. As I recall, he always had impeccable manners, all part of his charm.

"Alex, what ever happened to Tamika?"

"Tamika is great. She's in Houston working on her PhD in Psychology and getting married in April. Keith and I are flying down for the wedding."

"Send her my congratulations."

"I will. Maybe you should come to the wedding. Usually there are plenty of single women at weddings."

"If I can go as your date," he said with a smile.

"Nicholas!"

"I'm just letting you know how serious I am about this."

"But I keep telling you I'm with somebody else," I said looking into those brown eyes and hoping I was speaking the truth.

"At this moment, you are with me. Whether or not you want to admit it, that means something."

"But it doesn't mean I'm not marrying Keith."

Nicholas just smiled and ordered more coffee.

I excused myself and went to the ladies room. I called Keith to find out if we were going to see each other today. That was a no. He and his brother-in-law were going to be painting his parents' rental property.

I tried Stephanie next. She was either still in bed, or in or near a shopping center.

"So how's it going with Nicholas? I've been dying to ask, but I know how you can be."

"Yeah, I am a little funny about people giving out my personal information to men without my permission."

"Oh please, Nicholas isn't just any man. Plus, you're on your second date with him."

"And how do you know?" Was my sister in cahoots with Nicholas all along?

"Don't worry about that. Just enjoy it and call me back later with all the juicy details. Please have some juicy details!"

"Remember, little Sis, I am not you."

"I know that, because if the tables were turned, I would not be on the phone when I could be riding some fine ass dick right now."

I was still shaking my head when I got back to the table. My sister certainly had a way with words, but she was not wrong about the "fine" part. Would it really be all that wrong to spend some time with Nicholas just for this one day? I mean I wouldn't let things get out of hand.

We left the restaurant and went for a drive to nowhere, I thought. We ended up at the Jamaican store Nicholas's parents owned. I loved the Paxtons. They were always so sweet to me. Nothing had changed. They welcomed me like I was family. Too bad my own parents weren't as warm to Nicholas.

"Oh my goodness, child, we thought we were never going to see you again. Nicholas has gotten all of that foolishness out of him now. He will treat you much better."

"Mrs. Paxton, Nicholas and I are not together. I'm engaged to somebody else," I said showing my ring.

She looked confused. Mr. Paxton changed the subject by offering me some fresh baked goodies. I loved watching Nicholas and his parents interact. There was a lot of love between them. I enjoyed seeing them again and said so when we left.

When we got back in the car, I was the guilty party. I meant to kiss his cheek, but he turned and before I knew it, we were locked in a full blown kiss. I wanted him as much as he wanted me. This was crazy but I couldn't help it. Nicholas felt good to me even now, but I was not that kind of girl.

"My house is closer," he whispered.

"I can't," I said as I reluctantly pushed him away. "I'm sorry. Just take me home."

The ride was long and silent. I felt guilty about Keith and Nicholas. I was stupid to think I could do this without hurting anybody. Well at least I could put an end to it once and for all and get back to my drama-free life.

My plan to just get out and go inside was not to be. "Alex, you can scream all day and night about how you're marrying Keith, but your actions tell a different story about where your heart lies."

"You're right. I know better. I won't let this happen again," I said without looking at him and went inside.

Chapter 5

Nothing to do, but focus on doing the right thing. My guilty escapade was over. I hadn't really cheated on Keith. I could put it all out of my mind and concentrate on what was important.

At least Keith and I would have some time together on Sunday, even if it wasn't alone time. He picked me up for church. I greeted him warmly. I sensed a little coolness. I thought it was just about the premarital sex thing. After church, Keith still seemed a little quiet so I asked if anything was bothering him.

"I don't want to talk about it right now," he said and continued driving without looking at me.

"Is it something I said or did?"

"I said we will talk about it later, Alexandra."

Alexandra? I must really be in trouble. There was no way he knew about Nicholas. Keith had spent the day in a different part of the state... unless somebody had seen us together. I hadn't seen anybody I knew at breakfast or at the Paxton's market. I put it out of my mind and tried to look forward to dinner with Keith's family, hoping for a pleasant evening.

Patricia was there with her husband Bill and their three children. Keith's older brother AJ was also there with his wife Gloria. The elder Howards, Maxine and Albert, Sr., rounded out the group. Something was definitely up when we walked in. The house got quiet. Somehow, they must have known, but apparently, they were saving it for later. I guess I was going to be the after-dinner entertainment, or so they thought.

I offered to help clean up. It was decided the children could do that while the grown-ups talked in the living room. I waited for the drama to begin. As usual, Patricia was the one taking charge.

"Alexandra, we are a very traditional Christian family. We take marriage seriously. So it was a little upsetting to see you yesterday with somebody other than my brother, your fiancé."

I was really stunned. Keith just sat there while his sister attempted to humiliate me. I had no problem acknowledging my wrongdoing, but I would not be made a spectacle of. I stood up and said to Keith, "I'm going home. Are you taking me, or should I call a cab?"

"You're not going to address this?" Keith asked.

"Not here," I said and moved toward the closet to retrieve my coat. I could wait outside for my cab.

"No one said you had to leave." Patricia's arms were crossed, sanctimonious as hell.

I stormed out the door. Keith followed. Over my shoulder I screamed, "What the hell was that? Do you have to have your sister do your bidding for you?"

Keith yelled in return, "So I'm the bad guy? I wasn't the one sucking on somebody else's tongue!"

"Don't I know that!"

"So that means you can be a ho?"

Both of us were shocked at the sound of my hand connecting with his face.

Chapter 6

Keith rubbed the spot I had just hit, "Let's go."

"I'm sorry, but you shouldn't have called me a name."

I tried to touch his face, but Keith was having none of me at that moment. He waited until we were in the car before asking the question.

"So who was he?"

Why did I think I could hide it from him? I was stupid to ever let Nicholas come between us. There was nothing to do now, but tell the truth and see where it led. I wanted to have a rational conversation back at my apartment, but would that still be possible?

"Why don't we talk about it when we get there?"

"Fine," Keith agreed through clenched teeth.

I had managed to tick off two men in as many days. At this rate, I'd be alone very soon. How had I gotten myself into this pickle, and how would I get out of it?

If I was going to do battle, I might as well be comfortable. I changed out of my nice church clothes and settled into jeans and a sweatshirt. By the time I returned to Keith, he was sitting impatiently in a chair. Maybe I should have been more concerned with his feelings since I had kissed another man and then slapped my fiancé's face. But he'd called me a ho, so I took my time.

I settled on the sofa and motioned Keith to sit beside me. "Okay, what would you like to know?"

"His name, for starters."

"Nicholas."

"The same Nicholas who got you pregnant in college?"

"Yes."

"So how did you hook up with him again?"

"The day Patricia and Stephanie met me for lunch, he happened to be there too."

"And how did he just happen to get your phone number?" Keith's tone was becoming increasingly sarcastic.

"Stephanie took it upon herself to give it to him, without my knowledge or consent."

"Then how did you end up in a car kissing him?"

How was I supposed to answer that? Keith wouldn't like any explanation I gave. Should I just admit Nicholas is incredibly *fine* and he was paying some attention to me when Keith wasn't, so I succumbed to his charm? Keith's eyes were burning a hole in me so I just spit it out.

"I was aiming for his cheek."

Keith had the 'Are you kidding me?' look on his face. He wasn't buying it. I had to bare all if I expected to remain his intended. So I did. From the restaurant to the kiss, I made sure I included the times I tried to get Keith to spend time with me and he wouldn't. A little guilt can be useful.

Keith paced the floor for a minute trying to digest what I had said. "So it never went further than the kiss? You haven't slept with him?"

"No, I haven't."

"And you told him not to call you anymore or come over right?"

"I did."

Keith stopped pacing and stared right into my eyes. "What if he doesn't stop?"

I reached up for Keith's arm. "I think when we get married, Nicholas will know he's lost."

"So until then he still has a chance to win you back?"

"No, I'm saying Nicholas will eventually give up. He probably already has. I haven't heard from him since yesterday."

"Do you want to hear from him?"

I stopped him from pacing and led him to the sofa with me.

"Keith, this is getting silly. I am with you. I apologized for my wrongdoing, can we get past that and move forward?"

"I don't know if it's that simple. I should be able to trust my fiancée to be faithful. I'm going to need to pray about this."

"Shouldn't we pray together?" I asked as I took his hand in mine.

He yanked it back. "Would we be praying for the same thing?"

"How can you ask me that? I think that if the tables were turned, I'd give you a second chance. I would love you enough to forgive you for a minor transgression. Can't I have the same consideration?"

"I'm not sure how minor this is. Second, don't you think your first transgression was getting involved with him way back when?"

I was on my feet now, "Way back when? When I was in college? Before I knew you? Are you really going to throw that in my face? Amazing how that didn't seem to bother you when you wanted to sleep with me. Not to mention the fact that you did not come to this relationship innocent yourself, Keith. Now if you need some time to think, I can understand that. If you find that you can't forgive me, then I'll have to live with it, but don't think I'm letting you, or your family throw this up in my face all the time."

"I guess I need to go then and start thinking."

"I agree." I had some thinking to do myself.

"And while I'm doing that, you might want to get out your bible and study the word 'submission' instead of getting your clues from *The Real Housewives of Atlanta*."

Chapter 7

I thought I would have some down time after Keith left, but I was very popular with my relatives. First my mother called to check my sanity.

"Alexandra, what is wrong with you? Keith is every girl's dream man. He's a Christian, a hard worker, loves his family. He treats you like a queen, and you have the nerve to disrespect him by letting that devil touch you again? You are 25 years old, not some silly teenage girl. Act like it. Keith is a wonderful man. You need to thank God every day for putting him in your path and taking that heathen out of your life. Do you need someone to knock some sense into your head?"

I took a deep breath. "Mom, I have asked Keith *and* God for forgiveness. I am praying for a yes from both. I did the wrong thing and I know it. I promise I won't disappoint you again."

"I hope not. You were always the good girl, until you met that heathen and everything went to Hell."

My next caller was my sister. "You know what, Alex? You just got your out, and you need to take it. Keith and his family are sanctimonious asses. To hell with them. Go be with the man you really want."

"Keith is the man I want. Nicholas was never anything but trouble." I was beginning to sound like my mother.

"Why, because mommy said so? It's your life, do what makes you happy. Stop trying to please your mother. I have news for you—it's an impossible task."

"Stephanie, why are you so invested in this? You don't even believe in marriage."

"But you do, so if you're going to hitch yourself to someone forever, why not be happy? I think you're only with Keith because he's the 'right type'. Nicholas, on the other hand, revs your engine."

"I am engaged to Keith, I can't go backwards now."

"You can do back flips if you want to. Girl, you better stop trying to be 'Little Miss Perfect' all the time. Alex, I'm telling you, go for it. If you don't, you will regret it."

"Go for what? An affair? Once it ends, where will I be? Keith won't take me back."

"How do you know Nicholas doesn't want to marry you?"

"He never wanted to before."

"Things can change. Besides, do you really want to be related to Patricia? I mean if she was my sister-in-law, the first thing I'd do when she came to visit was poison her food."

Chapter 8

A few days pass before Keith calls me. He wants to meet for dinner and talk. I hope this is the beginning of us getting back on track.

Things got off to a rocky start. Keith was there first. When I reached the table, I took off my coat.

"You weren't cold in that?" he said.

"No, why would you think that?" I seated myself across from him.

"There's a lot of room between the hem of your dress and your knees."

"Long dresses make me look short," I said defending myself. I didn't think I should have to, but maybe Keith needed some more time to get over recent events. I was willing to overlook this petty complaint.

"Okay, we can talk about your clothes later. Right now I want to know where we stand. I've been thinking that I might be partially responsible for what happened. I was so caught up in doing the right thing that I might have gone overboard and ignored you in the process. I'm sorry," he said.

"Keith, I'm sorry too." He was making an effort. I needed to meet him halfway. "So I want us to spend more time together, in a Christian way of course. What do you think?"

I would be an idiot to let this man out of my life. He was stable and safe, exactly what I needed in a mate.

"I want that too. Sex was never the most important thing in our relationship anyway, so we shouldn't have any problems being together in other ways. I am a very lucky woman to have you in my life. I love you so much."

"I love you, too," Keith said and took my hand in his.

We ended up back at my apartment. We cuddled on the couch talking and watching TV until we fell asleep. I woke up around two in the morning.

I nudged Keith, "Hey wake up."

"What?"

"It's after two. Let's go to bed."

"No, I better go home," Keith said still sleepy.

"You're not even awake. I promise not to take advantage of you."

"Okay, you go to bed. I'll sleep out here on the couch."

I was too tired to argue. I slid out from the blanket we shared, kissed his forehead and went to my bedroom until it was time to get up for work in the morning.

Keith was just waking up when I came out of my bedroom the next morning. I offered to make him breakfast, but he declined and went home to shower and change for work. I couldn't complain since we had sort of spent the night together.

For a while everything was great. Keith and I were spending many evenings together, no worrisome ex-boyfriends calling to muddy things up, no meddling future in-laws around. And soon, we would go to Houston for Tamika's wedding. I thought things would continue blissfully.

I had always believed I was perfectly capable of planning my own wedding, so the idea of having a wedding planner or coordinator was unnecessary in my opinion. My future sister-in-law thought otherwise and pretty much coerced Keith into giving her the job. I'm a pretty even-keeled person, so I don't let a lot bother me, but Patricia was one of those people who would try the patience of the saintliest person. The incident on that Sunday was just one example of her character. I didn't want to fight with Keith about his sister. As long as it didn't happen again.

Keith's family was having a birthday party for his mother Maxine on Saturday. I should say *Patricia* was having the party— since all that was required of Keith and AJ was money and their presence.

The party was at Patricia's house. She did all the cooking and preparations. I have to admit the house was beautiful. It sat on a small lot in White Marsh, or Nottingham, Maryland, as some called it. The combination stone-and-brick structure was at the end of the street, almost demanding to be noticed. Cars were beginning to fill the driveway and street as we arrived. I noticed my parents were already there.

One of Patricia's sons answered the door. He took our coats and directed us to the family room. The house was decorated in beautiful traditional white furniture. It was spotless; I guess the trick was never letting anybody sit anywhere except the kitchen and family room.

Patricia looked up as we entered. She gave me the once-over, disapprovingly, of course. "Hi, Patricia," I said as Keith came in and hugged his sister.

"Keith, I'm surprised you let your fiancée out in that little skirt. She might catch a cold or something."

I have always thought it rude to be disrespectful to someone in their own home. This woman was testing me. I was here to celebrate Maxine's birthday. Maybe I could convince Keith we should move to another state once we're married. In any event, we would have to talk about his sister sooner rather than later. And I decided Patricia was fired as wedding planner, too.

I saw my Dad standing in the corner looking bored. "Hi, Daddy," I said giving him a quick kiss on the cheek. "Why are you all by yourself? Where's Mom?"

"She's over there talking to some church folk," he said pointing to the spot near the patio door.

"Hello, Mr. Charles," Keith said offering his hand.

The two shook. My father made Keith nervous for some reason. I don't think anybody made Nicholas nervous. *Oops, no Nicholas thoughts allowed.*

My mother saw us and came over. Keith got a hug, I got a greeting, "Hi, Alex, I was wondering when you would get here. Albert should be here soon with Maxine."

"Good, the sooner they get here, the sooner we can leave," my father complained. I felt his pain.

As far as I knew, this wasn't a surprise party, but you couldn't tell by Maxine's reaction. She acted like she had no idea what was going on. Did I ever mention the Howards' flare for drama? She hugged every guest as if she hadn't seen them in forty years, including her family and friends that she sees almost daily. Her exchange with my mother was no exception.

"Roberta, I am so glad you came. I can't believe how many people wanted to celebrate my birthday with me. I am indeed blessed to have so many loved ones." Then it was my turn to be noticed. "Alexandra, thank you so much for coming. I had prayed you would be here with us today." Maxine squeezed me tight.

Was that another dig from this family? Yeah, it probably was. Why was I surprised? Secretly they probably called me 'Jezebel'—and a few other names that weren't biblical. Hopefully, after the wedding things would get better. They had to.

We were finally able to leave, after Maxine had opened all her gifts. The family had pooled their money and purchased a mink coat for her. Maxine was very pleased. She put it on and modeled for a few minutes, then had one of her granddaughter's hang it up in Patricia's walk-in closet.

On the way home, I tried to bring up the subject of Patricia. "I don't want her involved in my wedding plans anymore."

"Why?" Keith asked, his voice brimming with annoyance.

"She's too overbearing. She doesn't know when to mind her own business."

"She just wants the best for us, honey. Patricia is like a second mother to me."

I knew the whole story of how Patricia took care of Keith when he was a baby. Shortly after he was born, their mother was diagnosed with breast cancer. While she was being treated, fourteen-year-old Patricia took on a lot of the responsibilities in the family. Luckily, Maxine recovered, but apparently Patricia didn't relinquish her role, especially where Keith was concerned.

"Keith, if you don't put an end to her interfering now, she'll never stop. She'll try to tell us when to have children, how to raise them, and on and on. I should be able to have as much of a stress-free wedding experience as possible. Your sister makes that *impossible*. She's fired."

"Wait a minute. How much of this is really about the wedding? Or is it more about the 'Nicholas incident'?"

"You're right. Patricia was always overbearing, but the 'Nicholas incident', as you call it, was a tipping point. The fact that she wanted to humiliate me in front of your whole family was more than enough to make me want to steer clear of her."

"Well, Patricia thought we could get everything out in the open that way," Keith offered, defending his sister as usual.

I could scream. "Why do you always do everything she wants? You are twenty-eight years old! Will your sister always make your decisions for you?"

"I didn't say she made the decision. I asked for her advice and I agreed. I do make my own decisions; otherwise we wouldn't be getting married," Keith said defensively.

"Well that just proves my point. If she doesn't want you to marry me, she has no business planning our wedding. You should have told me that a long time ago. Do you want me to tell her, or do you want to make it a joint effort?"

"I haven't agreed to it yet," Keith whined.

"She's not in our corner, so why should she be involved, Keith? She's out!"

"Okay, but I'm going to remember this when I want to do something that you don't want to."

"Fair enough." I was glad it was over. I'd take care of Patricia tomorrow after church and deal with the wedding people on Monday.

Stephanie had left a message—no doubt she was trying to find out how the party went. She could have gone, but she loves

Patricia even less than I do. I called her back to fill her in on my adventure.

"That's right. Fire the bitch! I don't trust her anyway. Your wedding might not even be booked dealing with her trifling ass. Not that I'd be upset if you didn't marry Keith, but that's another argument. And if she wants to see a short skirt, show up at church in one of my booty bests. Oooh, I can't stand that bitch! Doesn't this convince you even more that you don't want to be a part of that family? Think about it, what kind of babies will you have, with Namby Pamby as the Daddy, and Auntie Vulture in the family? I want to actually *like* my nieces and nephews."

"You will love my children regardless."

"Let's hope so," Stephanie said not very convincingly.

While we were talking, my phone beeped. I checked and it was Patricia trying to call me. "It's her," I said in disbelief.

"Namby Pamby couldn't wait to tell her what you said. Ignore her call. I'm on my way over. I want to be there when you tell this bitch where to go. Do not talk to her until I get there," Stephanie demanded.

"Alexandra, I wonder where you are at this time of night. My brother probably needs to be worried. Anyway, he told me you don't want me to be part of your wedding anymore. It's true—I do have some concerns about your commitment to my brother, but if he's happy with you so am I. If throwing me away will let you give him some peace, I'm okay with that. Please call me when you come home. I pray you're not out doing something that will embarrass our family. Be blessed, Patricia."

I played the message back for Keith, "You see what I mean. I was crazy to let this woman anywhere near our wedding plans.

It's going to take everything I have to let her be a guest. Just keep her away from me."

"Patricia can be a little overprotective of me. She really doesn't mean any harm."

I was more than a little annoyed with this man at this point. Apparently, Patricia could do no harm in his book. Maybe she was just echoing what Keith really thought, but didn't want to say.

"Okay, fine I'll see you in the morning."

"Goodnight. I love you," he said like that solved everything.

"Love you too," I said as I hung up, wondering why loving Keith was starting to feel like a chore.

Chapter 9

When Stephanie heard the message, she wanted to go to Patricia's house. "Please, Alex, can we just bitch slap her a couple of times? She deserves it."

"Stephanie, we don't have to resort to violence. I'll return her call and confirm that I don't want her involved with my wedding plans anymore and it will come to a civil resolution. Now if you can't behave, I won't let you listen to the phone call."

"You don't have to be condescending. Now call the bitch and tell her off."

"Hi, Patricia, it's Alex."

"Oh good, you got home safely," came Patricia's sarcastic response.

"I've been here since Keith dropped me off after the party. I just chose not to take your call. Anyway, there isn't much to say. You and I are not meant to work together on anything. Especially my wedding. So it's best if we stop trying just for Keith's sake. I do thank you for all that you've done so far," I said hoping Patricia caught the insincerity in my voice.

"I'm actually relieved to be free of the responsibility. I was never really comfortable being associated with *your* kind of wedding, but I was trying to be a trooper for my baby brother."

"I'm so glad we can agree on something. Take care, bye." I disconnected before Patricia could say anything else.

"Is that all I get for coming all the way over here?" Stephanie asked after I hung up.

I shrugged my shoulders. "I told you it would be cordial."

"You're no fun. You should have started with, 'Look bitch'. I wanted Jerry Springer and you gave me Mr. Rogers."

"Sorry."

"Oh well, maybe there's something good on TV tonight. Order us some food," Stephanie said plopping herself down on my sofa and reaching for the remote.

"It's late, what do you want to eat?"

"Pizza is fine."

I didn't intend to eat pizza that late but when it came I couldn't resist. The food was good and so was the company. Stephanie was always entertaining. She insisted on telling me her crazy thoughts about Keith's family.

"The sister is just too obsessed with Keith. It's one of two things—either she's his real mama, or even worse, she gave him his first taste of pussy."

I couldn't help laughing. "You watch too many reality shows, Stephanie."

"You can laugh if you want to, but I bet there's something stinky and kinky going on with them. I hope you don't come back from your honeymoon a basket case because Keith is calling out 'Patricia' or 'Sister' in bed."

"That will not happen."

"I'd take a closer look at her kids. One of the boys has a kinda small head. That's a sign of inbreeding."

"Stop talking about that woman's children."

"I'm just saying..."

Keith called the next morning before he came to pick me up for church. While we were talking, I was trying to tell Stephanie where something was.

"Who's there with you?"

I heard the accusations in his voice. That was maybe due. I ignored it. "Stephanie stayed over."

"Oh, okay. I'll be there in a few minutes."

Stephanie spoke my thoughts. "He probably thought Nicholas was here."

"Maybe for a second, but he believes in me."

"It would serve him right if he was. I should have told Nicholas to come over last night in my place, then you might have heard more hallelujahs and calling on the Lord than you'll hear in church this morning."

"Very funny," I said and lightly smacked the back of her head. "Will you still be here when Keith picks me up?"

Stephanie turned around with her fake fight pose. "Of course. I would be remiss if I didn't stay to greet my future brother-in-law on this fine Sunday morning."

"First, put your clothes on and second, behave!" I said and dismissed my conniving, yet loving, little sister

Keith seemed surprised that Stephanie was still here when he arrived. He spoke to her after kissing me. "Hi Stephanie, how are you?" Keith's back was to her.

"Wonderful. And you?" Stephanie shouted, as if he were blind and couldn't see where she was.

"Just great."

"Good. Alex and I had a great time together last night. There might even be some parts of it she can share with you."

"What does that mean?" Keith asked, taking Stephanie's bait.

"It means Stephanie is just being Stephanie. Let's go." I glared at my sister. "Are you planning on being here when we come back?"

"I don't know. I probably will wait until all you church people get off the road before I head out. I will be sure to lock up though."

Stephanie was up to something. What, I didn't know. I just continued to pray for tranquility in my life. I enjoyed the church sermon as usual. I socialized a bit with my family and others before Keith and I headed back to my apartment. We were going to change clothes and go do something on this nice afternoon.

We had a great day planned for this warm March day. We would go the zoo and walk around the park. I was looking forward to spending time with Keith without his meddling family. Perhaps tranquility *was* in my future.

Stephanie was gone by the time we got back. I absently hit the answering machine to listen to my messages. Keith was about to go change in the bathroom when we heard it.

"Alex, it's Nicholas. You called earlier? You didn't leave a message. Is everything okay? Please call me back, baby. I look forward to it."

Keith was livid. "You better explain this one and fast."

"I never called him."

"That's not what Nicholas said."

Is this how the rest of my life would play out? Always under suspicion?

I took a deep breath. "He said *someone* called, but nothing was spoken. Remember who was here this morning after we left for church? My baby sister."

Keith seemed to think that was plausible. "Yeah, she was. I guess she could have done that just to make me mad. Stephanie can be really childish."

"Let's not get on the sister train or we won't get anything else done today."

Keith smiled, "You might be right about that."

We were able to salvage our day. In four more months, Keith and I would be married and hopefully, all the strife we went through to get there would be over. Maybe even Patricia and I could be friends. Or at least tolerate one another.

Chapter 10

My bliss began to disintegrate as Easter approached. Having Easter dinner together had not been a big thing in my family since my maternal grandmother had died seven years ago. My parents and I pretty much went to church every Sunday, so that wasn't a big deal either. The Howard family apparently thought differently. They were to come together once again at Patricia's house for dinner.

"I'm not stopping you from going. I just don't want to go. Your family will have a better time without me."

"I won't. You were the one who complained about us not spending time together. This is time spent together. Also, remember I gave in about my sister and the wedding," Keith said hugging me from behind.

Well, he had me there. I could see this was some sort of tit-for-tat thing. I reluctantly agreed to go, but made it clear, I would leave if Patricia started up with me. All I could do was pray.

I did everything possible to make things go smoothly. I wore a dress that revealed only my arms from the elbows down and my legs below the knees. I didn't even wear any of my cute shoes; I settled for the comfortable low heels I typically wore to work. I was prepared to smile and be the submissive future Mrs. Howard everyone seemed to want me to be.

Patricia outdid herself with the Easter feast. She must have started cooking days ago. The table was filled with ham, a beef roast, baked chicken, greens, sweet potatoes, potato salad, string beans, corn, chocolate cake and apple pie.

Apparently to keep from making snide comments, Patricia chose to basically ignore me. She also had someone else to pick on, her husband's sister Candace. Candace lived in Pennsylvania, which usually kept her out of Patricia's claws. She was divorced with one teenage daughter, who luckily escaped her aunt by staying in Pennsylvania with her father and his family.

After Candace complimented Patricia on the dinner, Patricia ungraciously thanked her with, "If you knew how to cook, you might find a new husband."

Candace just looked at her. Nobody in the family said anything to Patricia, which is how things always went. *When Keith and I get married, will I be the one to always take her on? Or will I become like the rest of them?*

I was looking forward to going to Houston for Tamika's wedding. It would be a chance for Keith and I to be alone together for a few days. When I was doing some last-minute shopping, I called Keith to see if he wanted me to pick up anything for him.

"Alex, I've been thinking about it and I decided not to go."

"Why?" I blurted, louder than I should have.

"Lots of reasons. Tamika is *your* friend, not mine. I wouldn't know anybody there except you. Plus I could save those vacation days and have more for our wedding. And finally with all that time in close proximity, we might end up doing the wrong thing."

"But I want you to go with me. We've been planning this for months. We have the plane tickets, the hotel reservations. It's less than a week away. Why are you backing out now?" I asked. "Did your sister tell you not to go?"

He was annoyed that I said that. "I'm working, can we talk later?"

I was annoyed too. "Sure."

To his credit, Keith did come over later and try to explain his decision. All of his arguments fell on deaf ears. I offered my theory of why he changed his mind.

"I know your sister is behind this. She wants to get back at me about the wedding. Don't you see how manipulative she is?"

Keith rolled his eyes. "Don't you think you're a little paranoid about Patricia? She does have other things to do besides making your life miserable."

"I'm not so sure about that. But I am sure that she can do no wrong in your opinion. It's always me that's wrong. Is that how our marriage will go?"

"Our marriage will go fine once you start accepting that I am the head of the household, and stop challenging everything I say."

"Don't make this about me. I'm just trying to figure out why you're going back on your word. It seems odd that you didn't have any problem with going initially."

"I changed my mind. Don't make such a big deal out of it."

Well, if Keith didn't want to go, there was no way I could force him. I was disappointed but also in a way looking forward to being on my own and not having to please someone else for a few days.

Stephanie, of course, had plenty to say. "Perfect. Now you are free to do whatever you want. I bet we can find you a real date. Let's see what you're packing. No old lady dresses." Stephanie reached into my suitcase and removed the pale blue high-necked dress I'd packed. "It's warm in Houston. Let's make sure you have some short skirts, some shorts, a sexy bathing suit and some sexy undies."

"Why would I need sexy underwear when I'm traveling alone?"

"You never know who you'll run into—or up against—so you should always have on sexy underthings. I have so much to teach you about life."

The ride to the airport brought on another lecture about why marrying Keith was a mistake. "He doesn't trust you. I bet Patricia told him you're still seeing Nicholas on the side and Keith is setting a trap. How can you marry somebody who doesn't trust you?"

"Stephanie, that's just another one of your unsubstantiated theories. Remember when you tried to cause trouble with that phone call? Keith believed me when I told him I didn't call Nicholas."

"Maybe he did, maybe he didn't. None of that changes the fact that you shouldn't marry him."

"Can you imagine all the problems I would cause by calling off the wedding at this late date? Everything is set, purchased and paid for. Basically, the only things left to do are mail the invitations and show up for the ceremony."

"So even if you're making a mistake, you won't stop because it's too close to the wedding date? Are you saying you're willing to go through with a marriage to the wrong person, just because you don't want to cause trouble? I hope Tamika can give you a counseling session or two because you definitely need it."

"Shut up, Stephanie! I'm not you, remember? I care about consequences."

Stephanie was quiet the rest of the ride. Three whole days of not being judged by anybody... I couldn't wait. Maybe I'd never come back.

Of course I was kidding. I had to return. Everybody was counting on me to do the right thing. And with one exception, I always did the right thing.

⁂

The check-in process didn't take long at all. I settled in with a book while I waited for my flight to board.

"Miss Alexandra Powell? Please come to the ticket counter."

What's going on? I hope I wasn't getting bumped from the flight.

"Miss Powell?"

"Yes," I said nervously. "Is something wrong?"

"Oh no, not at all. We just needed to let you know your seat has been upgraded from coach to first class."

"Really, how did that happen?"

"I'm not sure, but the system shows you've been moved up. When they call for first class to be seated, I invite you to board immediately."

I was excited; I'd never flown first class before. I heard it was roomier and the drinks were free. I was one of the first to get on the plane. I settled into my comfy window seat and wondered if the seat next to me was going to remain vacant. That question was answered quickly.

He slid into the seat, like he owned it. "Hey, beautiful. How are you?"

Chapter 11

What could I do, run for the exit? Causing a scene was not my style. I just shook my head, "I'm great, Nicholas, how are you?"

"Wonderful, now that I'm sitting next to you."

"I can't believe you did this. Do you think in just three days you'll make me change my mind about marrying Keith?"

"It might not take that long. I'm not trying to convince you to do anything crazy, just to admit you never stopped loving me and that you should be my wife instead of the other guy," Nicholas said with those beautiful piercing brown eyes. They had swayed me not so long ago to do whatever he wanted. But I was older now; surely I wouldn't be so mesmerized this time.

"What if I ignore you?"

"I doubt you'll do that. I mean Tamika won't have time to hang out with you. You don't know anybody else here. You'll want somebody to talk to, have meals with, go swimming with," Nicholas said and then leaned closer and whispered in my ear, "And who knows? You might want somebody to make love with, too."

It was impossible to be angry with him. After dinner was served, I told Nicholas I was going to sleep until we landed in Houston. I don't know how much I slept but at least with my eyes closed I could avoid his seduction attempts.

My plan once we arrived at the hotel was to be rid of Nicholas. Of course it didn't happen exactly that way. I called Keith as soon as I got to my room.

"Hi, sweetie."

"Hi, how was your flight?"

"Great, not even a minute of turbulence," I said purposely leaving out my flight companion. "Too bad you couldn't come with me."

"Yeah, but you'll have fun even without me."

"And what will you be doing while I'm gone?" I asked expecting to hear about housekeeping, church, dinner with the family.

There was a long pause before Keith answered. Then he tried to explain, or should I say, justify things. "Well, it turns out I'm going to North Carolina with Patricia, Bill and the kids. They had planned to go all along and once they found out I had the same days off they asked me to go, too."

"What an amazing coincidence. Who exactly is supposed to be the fool here, Keith, me or you? Your sister knew we were coming to the wedding this weekend. Either you were gullible enough to fall for this, or you two were in it together and decided to punish me in some way for noncompliance with the Howard family rules of behavior. Either way, this just goes to show where I fit in your priorities. Have a wonderful trip, Keith," I said and hung up.

I was furious. I started pacing the floor and calling Keith and Patricia every name in the book. They had messed with the wrong girl. I plotted ten different ways to beat the hell out of both of them when I got home. What kind of man was I marrying?

Was the solution to my problems somewhere in the same hotel? What would it mean if I turned to Nicholas? Was I giving up on Keith? I tried to calm myself down. I called Tamika but she was busy. I couldn't call Stephanie; she would just encourage me to seek out Nicholas. And if my mother knew Nicholas was here, she would be on the next flight down.

I flipped on the TV and tried to focus on that. I wasn't very into it and decided to take a quick shower and go to bed. I had just come out of the bathroom when the phone in my room rang.

"Hello."

"Hey baby, I'm lonely. Can I come to your room?"

"No, Nicholas, I was just going to bed."

"It's only ten o'clock. I promise I'll behave."

I wasn't really sleepy anyway. "Okay, I'll meet you in the lobby in fifteen minutes."

How much trouble could I get into in the lobby? I traded my towel for a cute black halter dress and some matching sandals.

Why did he always have to look so good? Nicholas stood as I approached. He had on a casual white shirt with black pants. Why was I trying to remember what he looked like without clothes? We were in the lobby, no chance of anything happening here.

"I'm so glad you decided to join me. Do you want to stay out here or go sit in the bar?"

I could see the bar from where we were standing. It offered some privacy without the intimacy of a hotel room, so I chose the bar. We settled on a booth near the back.

"So whose idea was this? Yours or Stephanie's?"

"I'd say it was Keith's. He's the one who chose not to come with you. What kind of clueless A-hole turns down an invitation to be your date for anything?"

"What happens when we go home?"

Nicholas took my hand. "We live happily ever after together?"

"Why are you so sure we are meant to be?"

"Because when I look at you or simply think about you, I feel the love that I felt for you before the accident. When I'm with you, I feel it from you too."

"Do you know what kind of trouble I would cause if I called off my wedding now?" I asked debating whether to let go or not.

"I think the greater damage would be to marry the wrong man."

I pulled back. "Nicholas, how am I supposed to change my whole life like that? Go against my family and choose you over Keith? How do I know you want to be with me?"

"Alexandra Yvette Powell, I love you. I'm older and wiser. I want to marry you, not a year from now or even a month from

45

now. I want to marry you right now. But since I took out the marriage license in Maryland, we have to wait until we get back home."

I was stunned. I must have frozen with my mouth open for quite a while. This wasn't happening. "Are you serious?"

Nicholas took my hand again, "I would not be here if I wasn't."

"Even if you're sure about your feelings, how can you be sure about mine? What if my reaction to you isn't love, but is more about Keith not paying much attention to me?"

"I always looked at it this way. Keith is the safe choice. You said it yourself; he's your mother's pick. The last time your parents saw me, it was in a hospital room and it was my fault that you were there, so I understand their dislike for me. If I hadn't been so stupid, there would be no Keith." He was still holding my hand, and then added, "And I'm sure your next question is why didn't I try harder to keep you from leaving me."

I nodded my head, "Yes."

"Because I didn't think I deserved you then."

Suddenly, I thought we were in the wrong place to be having this conversation. I could definitely see myself crying at any moment, so I suggested we go to my room. I was fairly sure we wouldn't do anything other than talk.

Chapter 12

I sat in the chair by the bed. Nicholas turned the desk chair around facing me and continued what he had been saying downstairs. "The last thing you said to me was that you had given me everything—and I had destroyed it with my own selfishness. You were right. How could I ask you for anything else?" Nicholas looked more vulnerable than ever. "When I saw you again after all this time and then you told me you had forgiven me, I realized it didn't have to be over."

I was crying. I got up and walked over to his chair. "I'm sorry," I said and hugged him. "I was hurting and feeling guilty myself and I lashed out at you. I know you didn't intentionally hurt me."

Nicholas pulled me onto his lap and then I saw he had tears in his eyes, too. "If I could have spared you that pain by dying instead, I would have wanted it to end that way."

I felt like I couldn't breathe. I kissed his cheek and pressed closer to him. "No, I didn't want that ever." I didn't want to let go of him and I didn't. We held each other in silence for a long time.

Finally I got up. It was late, but neither of us wanted to separate. Silently, I picked up the remote and turned on the TV. I climbed on the bed and Nicholas followed me. I didn't stop him.

I think we were both a little worn from the conversation, not to mention the fact that it was after midnight by now. At this point, sleep was about all we could handle.

A few hours later I woke up. I felt Nicholas's arm across me, his soft breathing beside me. I felt content, like this is how it was supposed to be, but we were a long way from home, far from the normal distractions. Would our reality be the same?

The next time I woke, it was when the phone rang by my bed. Nicholas was stirring, too. What if it was Keith?

"Hello."

"Hi Alex, it's Tamika. I'm sorry I didn't get back to you last night."

"No problem, I understand," I said, oh so grateful that it was Tamika and not Keith on the phone.

"Look, Eric and I have some free time this morning. Can you and Keith meet us for breakfast?"

"Sure, what time?" I figured I'd explain Nicholas when we saw each other.

Once I hung up with Tamika, I turned my attention to my bed companion, who seemed quite content. "Good morning, we have a breakfast date with Tamika and Eric, so go get ready."

"Are you sure you wouldn't rather have room service?"

He's back! "Get out of my bed and out of my room please."

"What time are we leaving?" Nicholas asked as he reluctantly got up and put on his shoes.

"I'll meet you in the lobby in an hour."

"Okay," he said and then stopped at the door. "By the way, you look beautiful first thing in the morning."

Once the door closed, I answered, "So do you."

I chose hot pink this time. My linen two-piece set was a sleeveless top and short skirt with matching sandals with straps that snaked up my leg. As I was about to leave the room, I turned on my cell phone. I had two messages, one from my mother and one from my sister. None from my fiancé. The surprising part was, I wasn't upset about it.

Tamika was definitely surprised to see Nicholas instead of Keith. We exchanged hugs and sat down at the table together. "Obviously something has changed since we last talked, Alex."

"Please don't ask me to explain any of this, because I can't," I said honestly.

Nicholas bailed me out. "Check with her again after your honeymoon. She should have all the answers by then."

We had a nice time catching up. Of course there came a point when Tamika and I ended up in the ladies room talking. "I don't know how I got into this situation. Nicholas showed up and everything went haywire."

"So is the wedding off?"

"If I keep hanging around with Nicholas, probably so," I admitted for the first time.

"I can't tell you what to do, but you sure do light up when Nicholas is around. I only met Keith once, but I didn't see it with him."

"Is spark everything? Keith is a great person. He's involved in the church, he will be a good husband and father." It sounded good on paper. "The truth is, Keith does not equal drama. My parents like Keith and the wedding is in less than ninety days."

"All good points, but if somebody asked me why I was marrying Eric, my first response would be because I love him. You listed a bunch of things and never once mentioned love. Getting married should be about being with the person you want to spend the rest of your life with, not just someone your parents like. Now I'm not telling you who to marry, but if one man makes your heart flutter and he's not your fiancé, you might want to think things over before you get to the altar."

After breakfast, Nicholas and I were left to our own devices. We had fun walking around downtown Houston, exploring a city neither of us had been to before. We went to the Buffalo Soldiers Museum and some souvenir shops before heading back to the hotel. I continued to play with fire by going to Nicholas's hotel room. I sat on the chair while he opted for the bed.

He was just staring at me. "What?" I asked.

"I was just wondering, among other things, how to get that ring off your finger."

"So that's all you want me to take off?" I asked again playing with fire.

Nicholas patted the spot beside him on the bed. "All I require of you is to take off that ring. I'll take care of the rest."

I didn't move. "So if I don't take off the ring I can climb on the bed with you and watch TV with my clothes on?"

"Absolutely," he said patting the spot again.

I took the spot beside him and reached for the remote. I settled on one of the many judge shows. Nicholas sat quietly for about five minutes. "Does this remind you of the old days?"

"Very much so. You would invite me to watch TV in your bedroom, promising nothing would happen that I didn't want to happen. But you were always nuzzling my ear or sliding your hand up my leg."

"Like this?" he said, and started reenacting the old days. It was like that day in his car... except we were in a bed... and I wasn't pulling away. Nicholas was unbuttoning my blouse.

I looked at my hand. "I thought you wanted me to take the ring off first?"

"Oh sweetie, you misunderstood. I didn't put an order on things. The ring can be the very last thing removed if you want it that way."

Chapter 13

It had taken less than 24 hours for me to fall completely under Nicholas's spell again... or maybe just admit I was never really free of him. The ring was off and so was everything else.

Nicholas was taking his slow sweet time getting reacquainted with every part of my body. I had forgotten just how wonderful it felt to have him touch me and taste me like I was his life source. He hadn't gotten inside me with anything more than his tongue and fingers yet, but he had set off every nerve ending in my body. When he finally was deep inside me, I didn't want him to move at first. Four long years had passed since the last time our bodies were locked together in love and I wanted to savor every moment. Nicholas indulged me a little, then I loosened my grip so that he could get things done. And Nicholas always got things done.

One more thing I loved about Nicholas was how he was still engaged after the loving was over. Our bodies were exhausted and sweaty, but still touching. Back when we were having sex, Keith wasted no time retreating to the other side of the bed or putting his clothes back on. I was surprised that I felt more joy than guilt at being with Nicholas.

As much as I wanted to stay right where I was, I needed to go back to my room and call my mother privately. I didn't dare attempt that while looking at Nicholas's naked body. I reluctantly started to gather my clothes from the floor and get redressed. I finally escaped to the bathroom because Nicholas kept trying to remove every item I put on.

When I came out fully clothed, he was looking at the room service menu. I was hungry too. I told him what I wanted and left for my room.

"Hi, Mom."

"Well it's about time you got back to me. What have you been doing all this time that you couldn't call your mother and let me know you were alright? I hope it wasn't shopping. You have plenty of clothes—albeit some inappropriate—but you should be saving your money right now."

"I had breakfast with Tamika and Eric this morning. Then I went sightseeing and window shopping mostly. That was pretty much it."

"Well just be careful. I could smack Keith for not going with you. It's not good for a single woman to be all alone in a strange city. I don't know what he was thinking."

"He was thinking what he usually does, which is whatever Patricia tells him to think."

"Alexandra, you shouldn't be talking about your fiancé like that."

Here she was, my mother, taking up for Keith again. "Really, well my loving fiancé could not or would not accompany me to my friend's wedding, but he found the inclination and the time to accompany his sister and her family to North Carolina this weekend."

"Really? That isn't right. What did you do to make him change his mind?"

"Just being myself apparently isn't good enough for Keith... or you."

"Oh Alexandra, please don't start. I'm just trying to be helpful. It sounds like you either need a nap or some dinner. I'll let you go and take care of that. Love you, goodnight."

"I love you too," I said and hung up. I was smiling as I thought of how my mother would react when she finds out how I really spent my time in Houston. I grabbed a few things I might need in case I spent the night in Nicholas's room and went back.

⋞⋟

"That didn't take long. My name must not have come up."

"I can wait until we get home for all hell to break loose."

For the first time since I took it off, I noticed the ring sitting on the nightstand. What was I supposed to do with it now? I definitely didn't want to wear it, but I didn't want it staring at me either. I put it in my purse for the time being.

Our dinner finally arrived. I was hungry after all our earlier activity. I wanted to dig in. Nicholas insisted on showing me something first.

"I told you the first night that we got here, that I love you and I want to marry you and that I had gotten the marriage license, remember?"

"Yes."

"Close your eyes." I did. He took my hand, "Now open them." I did. "Alexandra, I love you. I want to be with you forever. I promise you will never regret one day as my wife. Will you marry me?"

Nicholas was taking a big beautiful diamond ring from a box and waiting for me to say yes.

"Yes, yes," I said and the waterworks started flowing. "I love you. I never stopped."

He slid the ring on my finger and dried my tears. We hugged and kissed for a while, almost forgetting dinner. Nicholas had ordered champagne for the occasion. We drank some and memorialized our moment with our cell phone cameras.

We spent the rest of the evening acting like teenagers who had just discovered sex. Apparently, it had been a while for both of us.

"I wish we could stay like this forever," I said feeling warm and satisfied curled up naked with my man.

"Me too, just like this with me holding you and kissing you and tickling you."

And he was doing all of the above. "Stop!"

And he did but started something else. When we actually did sleep, it was a very good sleep. The wedding wasn't until 2:00 p.m. the next day, so we thought we would have plenty of uninterrupted time together.

The phone rang. It was around 5:00 a.m. Why did the ring seem louder at that time? Nicholas answered, said something inaudible and passed the phone to me.

"Hello."

"Good morning, sister dear. I just wanted to see how things were progressing. I guess since you're in Nicholas's bed, things are going very well. Happy Fucking! I'll get all the details when you come home."

I gave Nicholas the phone to hang up. We went back to sleep. This time we weren't interrupted. Eventually we had to get up though. I convinced Nicholas we should save room service for later and actually venture out of the room for breakfast. This would be my first time outside the hotel room wearing my new ring.

During breakfast, Nicholas's mother called. He told her we were engaged. She wanted to talk to me. I hoped she didn't think I was a flake because when we had last seen each other I'd been engaged to another man.

"Alexandra, first of all..." *Oh God, here it comes.* "Welcome to the family."

I let out a breath of relief. "Thank you."

"I just want you to know that Nicholas really has his priorities right this time. He will be a good husband to you," Mrs. Paxton said. "And when the time comes, a good father too. I am so happy that you two have come together again—this time for good."

"Thank you so much, Mrs. Paxton, for your support."

"Call me Rachel, darling. 'Mrs. Paxton' is too formal for family."

"Okay, Rachel. Do you want to talk to your son again?"

"Yes, and we'll see you soon, sweetheart. Bye."

Nicholas and his mother chatted for another minute and then he turned his attentions back to me. "Well, you certainly have the seal of approval from my mother."

"Good, that means a lot to me, especially since the support from my side isn't going to be as strong."

"Don't forget Stephanie. She's definitely on our side. You know, you shouldn't worry so much about what other people think. Alex, you are a fantastic person who has chosen the best man to marry—one out of two tries."

I raised an eyebrow. "I think that was a compliment, so since I love you I'll just say thank you."

"Why would I say anything that wasn't complimentary to you? Get used to it. This is the difference between how a real man treats the woman he loves and how a *wanna be* acts. I, Nicholas Benjamin Paxton, am the real deal."

Later I opted to go back to *my* hotel room to get ready for the wedding. I told him I needed to be in a different room in case he was thinking about having a "quickie" before the wedding.

"You surely have me confused with somebody else because I do not do 'quickies'."

I was smiling as I left the room thinking about how often I got to an 8:00 class with no time to spare because of Nicholas.

Tamika's wedding was beautiful. It was a small gathering with only two attendants. The ceremony was held in the neighborhood church where Tamika had grown up, and the reception was in a hall on the outskirts of town with a perfectly manicured lawn and outdoor patio that allowed guests to mingle inside or out.

When we walked over to the bridal table, I flashed my big new diamond. Tamika couldn't help but notice the change in rings. "So I guess this means we made some decisions?"

"Yes," I said and stopped. This time I didn't try to explain myself. I was getting better. Hopefully, I'd feel the same way when I saw Keith and my parents.

After the wedding, we went back to my room, so I could pack up all my stuff for checkout the next day. I was surprised to see the message light flashing.

I thought for a minute it was Stephanie from earlier that morning, but it wasn't. It was Keith.

"Alex, I was thinking about you. I tried calling you on your cell and your room phone. I hope you're not still mad about the weekend. Where are you? Give me a call when you get this message."

I didn't want to talk to him, because what I needed to say shouldn't be said over the phone. On the other hand, it was rude to ignore him. Sometimes being a grown-up stinks.

"I just need to call and let him know I'm okay."

Nicholas made no effort to move. "Go ahead."

"Are you sure you want to stay while I do that?"

"Yep."

I prayed Keith's phone was off. It was not. "Hello."

"Hi, it's Alex. I just wanted you to know I was okay."

"Good, where were you all day with your cell phone off?"

I thought I noted the tiniest bit of an accusatory tone in his voice. Understandable, I guess. "The wedding?!"

"At eight o'clock in the morning? And that was the first call to your room phone. After I couldn't get you on the cell I finally left a message with the hotel."

"I guess showering and eating are prohibited acts in your book." I was getting more and more annoyed with this man. I needed to end the call because Nicholas was getting annoyed too and the last thing I needed was for him to make his presence known.

"I was just worried about you."

"Thank you. I am alright. I'll talk to you tomorrow when I get in."

Keith reluctantly accepted that and we hung up.

Nicholas had words of encouragement for me. "See, you survived it. And you never have to go through that again."

I loved having Nicholas's arms around me but it didn't change the inevitable. "I still have to face him to break things off. That won't be fun."

"But I'll be there with you."

I shook my head. "No, I have to do that by myself. I may have changed my mind about marrying Keith, but I still don't want to hurt him anymore than necessary."

"Well, I don't know how he will react to the news. I want to be there in case he tries something crazy."

I'd have to deal with that dilemma tomorrow. Right now I just wanted to enjoy the final hours Nicholas and I had alone before World War III broke out. We spent our last night as we had the previous one, making love.

"Can't we just stay here?"

"How long do you want to stay? Eventually I have to go back to work to support us."

"You can't work from home?" I teased as I played with his chest.

"How much work would I get done with you doing this?"

I pulled away. "You want me to stop?"

"Not at all. As you can see, I am not in my office at the moment."

"I certainly hope you don't sit around your office naked."

"I haven't yet, but if you want to come by one day…"

I climbed up on him. "That might be fun."

Chapter 14

Sunday morning came too soon. Just as the sun was up, the phone rang. Half asleep and thinking it was Stephanie, I crawled across Nicholas and answered.

"Hello."

"So is it appropriate to call you a ho now, Alex?"

Oh shit. "Keith, I was going to tell you when I got home."

"All this time I wanted to believe you when you said weren't fucking him."

"I know you're upset. I want to explain things. We can talk when I get home," I said, knowing there was nothing I could say to make things right for him.

"There isn't anything to talk about. I should have listened to my sister when..."

I cut him off. "I am not interested in your sister's opinion. Now I said we can talk when I get home. If you don't want to do that, then so be it."

"You should get an award for your act. You are the most deceitful woman I've ever met!" Keith yelled.

"Keith, calling me names won't change anything. If that's all you want to say, I'm hanging up."

"I think the least you can do is listen."

Nicholas took the phone from me. "Keith, this conversation is over. You got dumped. Take it like a man and move on," Nicholas said and disconnected the call. He then called the front desk and put a hold on all calls to the room.

"I'm sorry," I said.

Nicholas kissed me, "It's not your fault."

We tried to go back to sleep. Only one of us succeeded. I eventually gave up and took a shower. I went back to my room and listened to the other messages left by Keith. They were surprisingly nasty from a man who often said profanity was a sign of weak character. I erased them and made one last check of the room before going back to Nicholas.

He was awake. "Where did you go?"

"To my room, to make sure I didn't leave anything."

"Okay, well I'll take my shower and then we can have breakfast."

After we ate, it was time to check out. We got to the airport and turned in the rental car with plenty of time to spare. I was still a little anxious about what I would face at home. I'm sure my phone was blowing up with calls by now, if not from Keith, from his sister or my mother. I planned to leave it off.

As if he was reading my mind, Nicholas asked, "So what's our first stop? Your place, your parents' house... or my, sorry, *our* house?"

"I love the thought of *our* house, especially since I've never been there. So let's make that our first, last, and only stop for the night."

Nicholas had a very nice townhouse, not far from my ex sister-in-law-to-be's home. We could always move after we got married. Leather and dark wood seemed to be the decoration theme downstairs. Upstairs there was more of the dark wood in the master suite, with a very inviting king-sized bed. The master bath had a huge soaking tub that I could see myself enjoying many bubble baths in.

We went back downstairs for dinner. While he looked for something to cook, Nicholas played his answering machine. One call stood out.

"Good morning, Nicholas, it's Lisa. I hope everything was to your liking. Where were you? I'm used to waking you up on Saturdays. Talk to you soon."

Before I could ask, Nicholas explained. "Lisa is my housekeeper. She cleans twice a week for me."

"And how does she wake you on Saturday?"

"There's no reason to be jealous. I'm looking at the only woman I want to be with."

"You still haven't told me how she wakes you on Saturday?"

"I figured you'd be here on Saturday to see for yourself."

"I certainly will. What's her other workday?"

"Usually Wednesday, but sometimes she comes a day earlier or later."

"But she never misses the Saturdays."

Nicholas was actually laughing. "Not usually, but need I remind you that I was with you yesterday all day... not thinking about anything but you all day."

"Make sure Lisa knows this."

"Well, if we get married before Saturday, everybody will know."

"We can't get married that soon. We need to let people absorb the fact that we're a couple first."

"Okay, but the license is only good for sixty days, I'm not getting another one."

"Oh, so your love has an expiration date? If I don't marry you within sixty days, I lose out forever?"

"Not at all, you just have to do all the work—get a new license, buy the ring, do the proposing..."

"I have a sneaking suspicion that I could get you to change your mind. If I tried really hard," I said pulling Nicholas close to me.

Chapter 15

We had one last night of bliss before the onslaught of questions and accusations came from all fronts, so we made the most of it. Nicholas was returning to work today and I had one more day off. I dropped him off and took his car to my apartment. I would come back to pick him up after work.

My plan was to do laundry and make dinner. I also needed to return some phone calls. I put the clothes in the washer and dialed my mother at work. Maybe she was in a meeting, or she and my dad had played hooky for the day.

"Roberta Powell, may I help you?"

"Hi, Mom."

"Alexandra, what the heck is going on with you? Did you sneak off with that devil?"

"Nicholas and I are engaged," I said with much more confidence over the phone than I would have had facing my mother in person.

"Wasn't it just a few weeks ago that you promised me you wouldn't disappoint me again? You had a good and decent fiancé, why would you go back to the devil that nearly killed you?"

"I love Nicholas. I'm sorry. I wasn't trying to disappoint you."

"I have a meeting in two minutes, but we will talk about this again later."

I was off the hook for a little while. My next call was to my sister.

"This is not phone conversation. I'm coming over there right now," Stephanie said.

"Aren't you working?"

"How can I work when my little brother is sick?"

"What little brother?"

"The one I created to use when I needed to leave early for no legitimate reason. Little Carlos has been very sick lately, and the doctors are still trying to figure out what's wrong," Stephanie said as if we really did have a little brother. Sometimes I worried about her.

She arrived just as she said she would, practically panting for details. "Tell me everything from the moment you saw him on the plane up until you got home and I do mean everything, including when you first fucked him."

I ignored her crudeness and then told her what transpired over the last few days, highlighting the proposal and not answering specific questions about sex. I showed Stephanie my new engagement ring.

"Oh, that is so much better than that QVC daily special from the former fiancé. I bet you served up the pussy to Nicholas twenty different ways after he put this on your finger."

"I wish our parents were here so you would watch your language. You have the nastiest mouth, Stephanie."

She didn't pay me any attention and kept talking. "Well you're getting your wish. The parents will be arriving this evening."

"They're coming here?" I asked almost in a panic.

"Yep. Did you think Roberta Powell was going to let you get away with defying her and not confront you in the most dramatic fashion? And Daddy is coming along because he put out a ton of money for a wedding that isn't happening and he is collecting from all parties. Don't you just love our family?"

Oh well, I knew it would happen sooner or later. Better to get it over with now. I made Stephanie help tidy up. I was making spaghetti for dinner, so there would be plenty for all my dinner guests.

When I told Nicholas, he was unfazed. To help me out he would take the subway so I wouldn't have to drive all the way downtown to pick him up. I loved him for wanting to be a part of this madness.

My parents showed up around 5:30. My mother again wanted me to explain myself. I told her the same thing I had before, "I love Nicholas."

She was not accepting that. "Do I have to remind you he nearly killed you?"

"That was an accident, Mom. Nicholas has changed for the better. I really wish you would give him a chance."

"You can marry whoever you want to, but is somebody going to give me my money back that I spent on a wedding that isn't happening?" my father asked.

My mother was not happy about the interruption of her scene. "Charles, we are not worried about the money. Our concern is Alexandra and her foolish choices."

"Roberta, you might not be worried about the money but I am. Do you know how much we laid out? Did you get a dime from the boy's family? I sure didn't. I know they had plenty to say about how the money should be spent, but when it came to actually doing the paying, their hands were nowhere near their wallets."

While my parents argued, I snuck out to pick up Nicholas from the subway. In retrospect, I wished he had waited downtown.

"We can still run the other way," I told him as we pulled out of the subway parking lot.

"I'm ready for my grilling."

When we returned to my apartment, my family was still there. Apparently the fighting between my parents had stopped. My sister was taking the breadsticks out of the oven, while my father complained about the menu. According to him, spaghetti wasn't real food. My mother just looked annoyed at all of us.

Nicholas, maintaining his usual calm and confidence, walked in and greeted everyone. He gave Stephanie a hug and shook my father's hand. His toughest critic however, my mother, sat hands folded across her chest glaring at him.

"Here he is, the devil himself. Are you proud of yourself, Nicholas? Upsetting everything? Embarrassing this family?

Ruining Alexandra's prospects of ever finding a good husband again?"

"Mrs. Powell, I know my past behavior doesn't make me look too good in your eyes. I have apologized to Alex for that. She has forgiven me... I hope in time you can too. As far as husbands go, I plan to be an excellent one."

My mother rolled her eyes.

"When I proposed to your daughter, I promised she would never regret choosing me. My priority will be to make her happy, and in the midst of doing that I might make you proud as well. All I can do is try. I can only ask that you give me a chance, not necessarily for me but for Alex's sake."

I was moved by what Nicholas said. The question was whether it would have the same effect on my mother. She could be extremely stubborn. Roberta Powell had decided Nicholas was no good years ago; it wouldn't be easy to change her mind.

She still eyed him suspiciously for a few seconds before speaking. "Nicholas, apparently my daughter is easily swayed by your good looks and hidden charms. I am not so easily swayed. If you are Alexandra's choice, I have to accept that. But... I do not have to like or trust you just because she does. You have to earn those things from me. I doubt that I will ever find you to be the best choice for my daughter, but time will tell. So far you have gotten off on the wrong foot with your escapades in Houston. I hope you exercise better judgment in the future."

"Thank you, and I know I can change your mind about being the best choice."

My mother reluctantly accepted Nicholas's handshake.

I breathed a sigh of relief. The worst was over. My mother had not disowned me or shot my beloved. Now I could feed these people and get them out of my apartment as soon as possible.

Once we sat down to eat, my father started in again. "Where's the real food? Dinner is supposed to be chicken, pork, or beef with some vegetables and dessert. How did you come up with spaghetti, Alex?"

"I like spaghetti," Nicholas offered.

"Don't tell her that or you'll get it every night for dinner."

"Daddy, this is the twenty-first century. Some nights Nicholas will cook, and sometimes we'll go out for dinner."

"Going out is expensive. Nicholas, what kind of money do you make?"

I was embarrassed by my father's questions, but Nicholas felt the need to open up. He answered, "Last year, just over six figures. This year, with my bonus and promotion it should be even better."

"That's real good money. You think you can help me out? I mean, you are the reason the wedding was called off. Why not help cover the damages I'm out?"

"Daddy, don't ask him that," I said mortified.

"The only reason I came over here was to get reimbursed," my father said unashamed.

"Mr. Powell, I can't offer you any help at the moment because it might look like I was trying to buy your daughter. Now if you ask me again after we're married, I might be able to do something for you."

"You can get married tomorrow. I can wait until the end of the week to get my money."

"I have no problem with that, but Alex gets to set the wedding date." Both men shared a chuckle.

"That's right, Daddy. I can't guarantee you this week." *But soon*, I thought to myself. Before Nicholas realized what he was getting into.

Chapter 16

I still needed to return Keith's ring. Of course Nicholas disagreed with me on how to accomplish that.

"Just mail it or drop it off at his parents' house."

"Don't you think that's a little impersonal? What if Keith wants to talk?"

"About what? He knows he was dumped. What's left to talk about? He probably doesn't even want his cheesy ring back. I definitely don't trust him to be alone with you."

"I appreciate you wanting to protect me, but I think I should handle this by myself."

"Didn't we agree already that if he came over, I would be here too?" Nicholas asked.

"That was before he knew we were together. Now he's had time to digest that and calm down."

"Alex, I'm not letting you be alone with this guy."

I was not at all comfortable with Nicholas and Keith being in the same location. I let it go because I could call Keith from work tomorrow to try to resolve this. I put it out of my mind and had another wonderful night with Nicholas.

The next day I went back to work. My plan was to get Keith to meet me somewhere for lunch so I could give him back the ring without him and Nicholas colliding. I called, but Keith didn't answer. I guess I'm no longer on his favorites list. Well maybe he'd call me back soon.

Of course Keith didn't call me until a few days later when Nicholas and I were on our way to the movies. That meant my plan to keep the two men separated had fallen apart. Keith said he would come by after work on Friday to pick up the ring.

Friday came but Keith never showed. I called but he didn't answer. Nicholas was ready to give up, but I was still willing to give Keith the benefit of the doubt.

On Saturday morning, I got to meet Lisa. Her special wake-up for Nicholas was vacuuming the hallway outside his bedroom before 8:00 in the morning. I suggested he stick with an alarm clock.

"What are you doing?" Nicholas asked as I got out of bed.

"Going to meet your housekeeper," I said. I slipped on my robe and went to the door.

She's fired. Fired, I said to myself, looking at the young blonde happily vacuuming the hallway. She was listening to her iPod and was startled to see me.

"I'm sorry. I'm not used to seeing anybody come out of Nicholas's bedroom. I'm Lisa, the housekeeper," she said offering her hand.

"I'm Alex, Nicholas's fiancée," I said thinking, *Good. Nicholas had not been bringing a lot of women home. And you won't have to get used to me, because as soon as I become Mrs. Paxton—if not sooner, you skinny white girl—you're history.*

I went back to Nicholas after assessing the housekeeper and deciding her future. "So are you satisfied that Lisa is only my maid?"

"She's fired."

"Alex, as lady of the house you will certainly have the right to fire her, but can you at least tell me why?"

Nicholas was not stupid. He knew why this girl had to go, but if he wanted me to spell it out, fine. "Because I don't want some young thing sniffing around my husband."

"Don't you get the tiniest bit of pleasure from seeing a white woman clean for us?"

"There are no old white women who could do it?"

"I never tried to find one. Lisa left fliers on doors all over the neighborhood. I hadn't really thought about having a maid until then. I called her, she came over for an interview and I hired her.

She does a good job and our relationship is strictly business. Can't I please keep my white maid?"

"Nicholas, I'm sure they have agencies with maids of whatever age and ethnicity we choose. I'll be happy to go on the internet and do some research."

"I guess it's a good thing I'm marrying a resourceful woman. I just hope she's as resourceful at setting a wedding date."

"That's already done, too."

"Great, are you going to let me know? Or is it a state secret?"

"I'll tell you five seconds after you fire your favorite white maid."

"I have to let her go now? Can't we wait for the replacement?"

"We can do the housework for a couple of weeks until we find someone."

"We? I was perfectly happy with Lisa doing the housework. I don't know why I should be inconvenienced for any length of time because my lovely wife-to-be has issues."

"Wasn't it just a few days ago that you were telling my family about how making me happy was your number one priority? Now I ask for one little thing and you give me flack. Was all that just talk, sweetie, baby, honey, love of my life?" I said as I crawled onto his lap.

"I meant what I said. I'm just being practical." Nicholas kissed me. "The less time we spend housekeeping, the more time we have for other things." He then began demonstrating what he meant by *other things*.

"Wait," I said pulling away. "The rule is fire the girl and then we can play."

"Shouldn't we let her finish for today first?"

"I guess that's only fair, and you should give her a nice severance check too," I said. I wasn't totally unsympathetic.

Lisa was history by 11:00. I was happy. Nicholas was happy.

I told him we could get married Memorial Day weekend. At least with a long weekend we could have a mini-honeymoon— and the date was before the license would expire.

Chapter 17

There was still the ring issue to be resolved. I decided to call Keith once more. Now, I was just irritated about the whole thing so if he and Nicholas had words, so be it. He actually answered the phone this time.

"Hello."

"Hi, I'm just calling about the ring again. I waited until after ten last night and you never called or came by. Do you want to do this in person or should I just drop the ring off with your parents or in the mail?"

"You didn't get it in the mail or from my parents, did you?" Keith barked. I couldn't argue with that. "Why are you in such a hurry to get rid of the ring? Does it make you feel guilty?"

"Keith, I know you don't like me much right about now, but this isn't helping matters. We can have one last heart to heart where you can politely tell me what you and Patricia think of me, pick up your ring and be done with me forever. You will be free to find the right woman to share life with. Doesn't that sound good?"

Nicholas had little faith that Keith would actually show up this time either, but just in case, he was there. He promised to stay in the bedroom and not intervene unless I screamed bloody murder. I just hoped Patricia would allow Keith to do this by himself.

This time Keith showed up. And he was alone.

I wanted to smooth things over as best I could. Despite what had happened, I didn't hate him—but I couldn't speak for Keith. We sat down and talked it over.

"I feel like I need to tell you I was not deceiving you the whole time."

Keith's lip curled in disgust.

I tried to ignore his facial response. I plowed on so he wouldn't have a chance to interrupt. "I didn't invite Nicholas to Houston. He surprised me on the plane. Yes, I did spend time with him and things did progress." But I didn't want Keith to think that he never mattered to me. "I really did care about you, Keith, but Nicholas and I are just meant to be. I'm sorry it took me so long to realize it... and that you had to get hurt in the process." I gave him the ring box.

Keith relaxed a bit. "Thank you for that. I guess it's best that you found this out before we got married. I wish you would have known before I bought the ring..."

"Yeah, that would have caused a few less problems. Well, you are free now to relax and see who's out there for you. You know there are women in the church who might want a chance now that you're single again."

Keith smiled, "Really? I guess I better open my eyes a little more."

"And one little piece of unsolicited advice. Do not let Patricia dictate your life—your romantic life in particular. Keith, you are a wonderful man with a lot to offer, but by letting your sister control you, that image gets skewed. No woman will accept being married to you *and* your sister."

"Thanks for the advice. I'll keep that in mind," Keith said and stood up to go.

I gave him an uncomfortable hug, we wished each other well and he left. I closed the door and breathed another sigh of relief. That chapter in my life was over. Now all I had left to do was plan my new wedding... or rather, courthouse visit. That should not take long. Nicholas was responsible for planning our short-notice quickie honeymoon.

Our next step was letting the family know we had picked a date. We went to see my parents first. Their response was mixed. My father was still hoping a check from Nicholas was on its way, so he wasn't thrilled about waiting three weeks. My mother was not yet completely sold on Nicholas, but decided if we really were getting married, the courthouse would not do.

"Alexandra, you should not get married without a place for the Lord in your wedding. This is happening very fast, but you still need to be married by a minister. Preferably in church."

"Mom, how can we get that done in three weeks?"

"Leave it to me. I'll talk to Reverend Raymond and see if he can do it, or one of the associate ministers. If they can't hold it in the church, we'll have the ceremony here. I always thought I would have two beautiful weddings, because I have two daughters. But Stephanie is a lost cause. So it all falls on you, Alexandra, to give this to me. And I don't want to hear anything but 'Yes, Mother' from you. Is that clear?"

"Yes, Mother," I said since there was no point in arguing with her about this. If I didn't let her have her way, she would remind me for the rest of her days on this earth about how I'd denied her this moment. Sure, I had stood my ground about who to marry—and I had stood my ground about the maid—but this battle I didn't need to have.

Telling Nicholas's family was so much easier. There were no demands. They just wished us well and wanted to know what they could do to help. I was really looking forward to becoming a part of this family.

Another demand from my mother was my attendance at church that Sunday. It was Mother's Day, and she said she was getting tired of Keith's family's snide remarks about me being whispered throughout the church, so I needed to show up with my head held high.

I was also told I could bring Nicholas if I wanted to, if he wasn't afraid to go.

Nicholas and I arrived in time to slide in on the row behind my parents and say hi before the service began. Of course Patricia, Keith and the rest of his family were seated up front, so it took a few minutes before they noticed our presence. I could feel the glare from Patricia several feet away. I'm sure this self-proclaimed Christian woman was feeding Keith as many hateful things about me as she could think of while she was supposed to be worshiping the Lord.

After the service ended, my mother wanted us to wait while she had a word with the reverend. We stood outside with my father. Some people came over to say hi and meet Nicholas. Most were pleasant, some snide. The Howards were outside, too. The ringleader decided to approach as the others waited.

Patricia was decked out in her Sunday best, complete with hat to match the lavender suit she wore. She smiled in her most insincere form and looked us up and down before speaking. "Well, this must be the infamous Nicholas. I only got a brief glimpse of you that other time I saw you with Alexandra. I just came to tell you I am so glad you two came to church today. I would hate to think you were staying away because of your sins. You know the Lord forgives all sinners if you ask and repent."

Nicholas set her straight in a hurry. "You are so right, because I swear you look just like one of the ladies that used to hang outside my parents' store in the evening, trying to pick up men. It's really nice to see you found the Lord."

Patricia was still trying to find her words when we were summoned over by my mother to speak to the reverend and one of his associates. My father gave Nicholas a high five for the quick comeback.

"Hello, I'm Reverend Raymond and this is my associate minister, Reverend Williams," he said and each shook hands with Nicholas. "I hear you are the new intended for Sister Powell."

"Yes sir, I am definitely the one who is marrying Sister Powell."

"I must say, Sister Powell, you are glowing in a way I did not see when you stood with Brother Howard."

I heard my mother gasp. Why did the minister have to say 'glowing'? *I hope Mom doesn't think I'm pregnant again.*

"Of course the Lord does work in mysterious ways," he continued. "So he may have been foreshadowing what was to come. Anyway, Sister Roberta Powell says you two have set a wedding date and that you want to marry in the church."

"Yes, if it's possible," I answered. "I know you have a busy schedule and this is extremely short notice."

"With the Lord's blessing, many things are possible. Unfortunately, I have another commitment that day, but Reverend Williams is available."

The associate minister spoke up. "I hope you're not too disappointed that Reverend Raymond won't be able to perform the ceremony. I haven't officiated as many weddings as he has, but of the few I've done, all the couples are still happily married."

Nicholas tightened his arm around my waist. "That's good to hear, Reverend. Alexandra and I plan to keep your streak going."

Chapter 18

Next there was dinner with my family. Nicholas had a previous engagement. I didn't tell mom he preferred golf over her.

The table conversation went smoothly enough; it was the ladies room conversation that made me blush. Stephanie had gone with me. There was a line, so she took the opportunity to make sure I knew I owed her for getting back with Nicholas.

"Every now and again, while you're climbing Mt. Nicholas, you should take a second and thank me, because without my hard work, your sex life would consist of you staring at the ceiling while Keith is huffing and puffing for all of thirty seconds. I saved you from becoming a permanent missionary—and I don't mean the ones who bring Christianity to third world countries."

"Stephanie! We are in a public place," I tried warning her to no avail.

"It's Mother's Day. Most of these women have kids, so I'm sure they are not unfamiliar with dick. I hope after you get married, Nicholas feeds it to you enough to loosen you up some. I would hate to see you lose your husband because you have no *freak* in you."

"Have no fear. Nicholas is very satisfied with me in every way."

"I certainly hope so. Because I need to get back to getting myself laid, now that I've safely freed you from the clutches of the pussy-whipped... and his big pussy sister."

I hoped once we rejoined the others, Stephanie might fade into the background, but no. Mom complained as soon as we returned to the table. "You two were gone so long, I was beginning to think you'd left."

"There was a long line," Stephanie said, "plus I needed to remind Alex how grateful she should be to me for getting her back together with Nicholas."

I couldn't resist teasing my baby sister. "Well, I was going to name my firstborn after you..."

Stephanie put up her hands. "Sorry. Already reserved that name for *my* baby."

"So you do plan to get married some day?" my mother skeptically asked.

"Of course not," Stephanie answered. "My plan is to have four children by four ethnically different men. I want my own small international group."

I could see my mother's jaw clenching.

"Stephanie, that is the most ridiculous thing I've ever heard! Why would you want to intentionally have children by different men? You were not raised to live such a crude life. If you try to do something like that I'll have you put away," my mother warned, as if she could stop her youngest daughter from doing anything.

"Roberta, don't get yourself so upset. Stephanie is just messing with you," my father said, then turned to his youngest. "This is Mother's Day, you are supposed to honor your mother, not upset her."

"Sorry," Stephanie said with no conviction.

"Can we just pretend we're a somewhat functional family—at least until after the wedding?" I pleaded.

It was outings like this that made me long to move out of state.

It was also why I refused to let my sister have the bachelorette party for me. Stephanie would hire male strippers for sure.

Chapter 19

The lease on my apartment would be up soon. I wanted to be cleared out before the wedding if possible.

Nicholas usually helped me in the evenings. We were putting things in three categories, one for the stuff I was taking with me, one for things I was giving away, and one for things I was throwing out. I found it hard to part with some even though I had no use for them anymore.

My future husband tried to put it logically. "It's broken, Alex. What good is it?"

I looked at the chipped plate and back at Nicholas. "This is from the first set of dishes I bought when I got my first apartment."

"Okay, but you have other dishes and so do I. Can we put this in the trash?"

I let him toss some stuff. I also made a note to pack while he was elsewhere since Nicholas was less sentimental. In retrospect, I probably should have taken his advice and tossed everything or gave it to goodwill and started over, but no I had to go back to the apartment.

I was busy sorting through things when I realized I had run out of tape. I was gone less than ten minutes and didn't notice anything was wrong at first. I opened up one of the packages of tape and started closing boxes.

"Hi, Alex."

I was startled because when I left there was no one in my apartment and because there was no reason whatsoever for anyone to be there. Then I suddenly remembered I had never gotten my key back from Keith. But then he had never shown up unannounced before either.

"Hi, Keith. What are you doing here?" He looked like he hadn't changed his clothes or shaved.

"I just thought I'd come see you. I don't think we really had a chance to talk the last time I was here. You seemed like you were in a hurry to get rid of me. Maybe you were trying to get to him sooner."

"I'm sorry you felt that way. I just wanted to end things as painlessly as possible," I said feeling even more uneasy about this man standing in my apartment with his hands behind his back. Did he have a gun or a knife? Maybe I could make my way to the door.

Keith was slowly walking toward me. "How was it going to be painless? You promised to be my wife and in a matter of days you accepted another man's proposal. You flaunted him in front of me at church, in front of my family and friends. Did you think that wouldn't hurt me, Alex?" I did try to make it to the door, but so did Keith. He blocked my path. "We haven't finished talking yet, Alex."

"Keith, this is getting a little scary. Do you really want to do this?"

"I know what I'm doing. Have a seat, Alex."

When I resisted, Keith pushed me toward the sofa. This was a side of him I had never seen before. "Keith, why are you doing this?"

"Because I want you to know that you can't just throw me aside like I'm nothing. We were a couple for two years. You said you loved me. I love you. Now you tell me it was all a mistake? I want you to explain it all to me from the beginning. Once I understand what went wrong I'll leave and never bother you again."

I thought if I went along with him, he would do as he said and leave. I still couldn't tell if he had any weapons. I might need one to get past him. I prayed it would not come to that.

"Well, you know I saw Nicholas again—for the first time in years—a few months ago."

"No, not that. I want to hear about before, when you first met him."

"We met at frat party when I was nineteen."

"And how soon did you sleep with him?" Keith asked with his eyes fixated on mine.

"You don't really want to talk about this. Let's talk about you and how much you have to offer."

Keith grabbed me off the sofa and turned me toward the kitchen.

I felt his hands digging into my shoulders.

"Look," he screamed. "Do you think I'm playing with you?"

That's when I saw that the phone cord had been cut. The situation was a lot worse than I thought. I had to find a way out. My cell was in my purse. I had told Nicholas I'd meet him at his house later.

"When did you first sleep with him?!" Keith shouted.

"A few months later on my birthday. Nicholas took me to New York for the weekend."

"Was he using drugs then?"

"Not that I know of."

"When did you find out?"

"A year or so later."

"But you stayed with him knowing he was a drug addict. You even got pregnant by him. *A drug addict?* I never even smoked a regular cigarette and I'm not good enough for you. How is that, Alex?"

"Keith, I never said you weren't good enough for me," I said hoping something would loosen his grip. "It just wasn't meant to be for you and me. There's a woman out there who is perfect for you. I'm sure it won't take you long to find her."

"Of course you would say that, but what do you care? You have him. What's better about him? Is it the sex? Is it better with him?"

I could see my phone vibrating from the outer pocket of my purse. I prayed somebody would know something was very wrong. Until then, I had to placate this crazy man.

"Come on now, this isn't you. Where is my strong Christian man? We both know I don't measure up to *your* standards. You can do so much better. Count your blessings that you didn't marry me." I searched his eyes for some sign that he was hearing me, but his hands still held tight. "I'm not the woman you want raising your children. Think about your future, your career, your family. You don't want to jeopardize all of that by doing something you'll regret. If you leave now, nobody has to know you were here," I said terrified that this might be the end of me.

"I'll leave when I'm ready to leave. We're just talking. I haven't done anything to you."

"Keith, you're holding me and preventing me from moving. That is something."

"You used to like it when I held you," he said and started kissing my neck.

I tensed as the stubble from his chin scratched me. I started crying, "Please don't do this. I did love you once. Don't make me hate you now."

Keith stopped long enough to ask, "Isn't this how he got back in your good graces?"

If I didn't do something right now, I wouldn't get another chance. The only parts of me free to move were my legs, so I made the most of it. I slammed my heel as hard as I could into his foot. The pain made him release me long enough to get to the door.

Unfortunately, before I could unlock the deadbolt, Keith came behind me and pulled my feet from under me. I fell face down on the floor.

Keith held me down and yelled, "Stop moving!"

I was still fighting. Then I started screaming. The struggle seemed to go on forever until there was a knock at the door.

"Ms. Powell, this is Baltimore County Police. Are you okay?"

"No! Please help me!"

"Leave us alone!" Keith screamed just as the door came flying open and a whole host of cops came in and pulled Keith off me.

Some officers handcuffed him and took him outside while others questioned me. I could see my sister running in as I was being questioned.

"Alex, are you alright?"

We hugged each other tightly. "I am now. I was so scared." I started crying again.

Chapter 20

I still had to talk to the officers so it took me awhile to comprehend how the police ended up kicking in my door. By the time I found out, I was surrounded not only by my sister, but also Nicholas and my parents. I had to relive the nightmare again before the police let me leave.

Apparently I had my sister to thank once again. Stephanie had decided to see if I had anything she might want left in my apartment. When she called my house and got no response she tried my cell and when that went straight to voicemail she tried Nicholas. When he said I wasn't with him, she called our parents and then decided to drive over. She saw my car in the parking lot and recognized Keith's car farther down. She almost knocked on the door when she heard the struggle but then called 911 and everybody else.

Keith was being led away. "Alex," he screamed. "Alex, I love you!"

It was very unnerving to think I once had feelings for such a disturbed person.

"Chances are, Miss Powell, he's going to be charged with false imprisonment and assault. Here's some information on getting an order of protection."

I felt sorry for Keith, but he had brought this on himself. Hopefully he would get some counseling.

My family fussed over me. My parents wanted me to spend the night at their house. Nicholas said he would take care of me. I ultimately chose to go with Nicholas. I just wanted to forget about what had happened. I knew he would see that I got the peace and quiet I sought.

Nicholas ran a bath for me. Once I got into the warm bubbly water, I couldn't help thinking about what had happened. Would

Keith have raped or killed me? How could I not have known he had that much violence in him? How much of it did I trigger by leaving him? How would this affect everybody? Would Keith go to jail?

⁊⁊⁊

The next morning, Nicholas made breakfast. I sat at the table in my nightshirt while he dished up eggs and bacon.

"Thank you, sweetie," I said. "Do you have time to take me to get my car after breakfast? Or maybe just drop me off at work?"

He looked surprised. "What? Don't you think you should take the rest of the week off? After what happened yesterday?"

"I appreciate your concern, but I can't let Keith control what I do."

"Okay, but what if I need you to take a day?" Nicholas moved behind me and put his hands on my shoulders gently.

I could easily spend the day just with him.

A few hours later, our afternoon was interrupted. We heard the doorbell ring. I stood up.

"No, I'll take care of it," Nicholas said as he reached for his sweatpants and t-shirt.

"I'll go get dressed."

First it was the police. The detectives wanted to follow up on what I'd told the patrol cops the day before. Then my mother showed up, still dressed in her black suit for work.

"I didn't know he was crazy!" she said and then turned to Nicholas. "I guess you might not be so bad after all. At least you never attacked Alexandra."

I suppose that was about as much of an apology as Nicholas was likely to get.

Reverend Williams showed up next. He spent more time comforting my mother than he did me. She was still very upset about what had happened.

"But he's from a good Christian family. They come in and go straight to the altar and pray every Sunday. His mother never told me he was like this. I can't believe I trusted my firstborn daughter to that psychopath."

The reverend put his arm around my mother. "Sister Powell, don't blame yourself. The devil manifests himself in many ways."

Stephanie also called to check on me. I thanked her again for saving me.

"You are so welcome. You're my only sister. I couldn't let some maniac kill you. Plus, all my good deeds should get me something tangible in the short run, like a new wardrobe, a car, a down payment on a condo, something like that."

"Maybe I can squeeze out a couple hundred?"

"Oh no, your life is worth much more than that. Ask your fiancé to give me a reward."

"Between you and Daddy, Nicholas will think we're all money grubbers," I said. At least Stephanie hadn't changed.

"Please. I'm sure he's used to being hit up for cash. Danielle probably asks for money all the time."

"Danielle is nothing like you, sister dear."

"Don't be so sure. Just because she's all quiet around you and her family doesn't mean that's how she is all the time. She and I have been known to be in the same haunts, and let's just say there is another side to your future baby sister-in-law—not that I said anything though."

"Okay, well thanks for the info. You have a good evening, Stephanie."

"You can rush me off the phone for now, but I am my father's daughter. I will ask about my reward again and again until I am properly compensated."

"I love you too, Stephanie," I said to my crazy little sister, who was my hero in this situation.

She might have still been talking when I hung up. For a brief moment, I wondered if she was right about Danielle. Did anybody really know anybody? I was more than sure that I knew

Nicholas and how wonderful a man he was. In fact I went to find him.

He was in his office, adjacent to the bedroom. "Am I interrupting you?"

"A pleasant one. I'm almost finished anyway."

"Good, because I wouldn't know what to do in that big bed without you."

Nicholas's eyes lit up. "We can't have that. If you could stand right there at the door looking beautiful, I will finish this report and accompany you to bed and we can decide what activities to pursue once we get there."

I love the way he spelled out his plans. I did as I was told and true to his word we were in bed in a matter of minutes. I made sure Nicholas knew how much I appreciated him for the man he was. I was so lucky that he came back into my life.

Later I verbalized my thoughts. "I love the way you handle things. I think it's your analytical mind that makes you assess the situation and formulate your plan before acting on it. You never once talked about getting revenge on Keith; instead you concentrated on what was best for me and for us and I really appreciate that."

"I told you, you are my priority. That doesn't mean I didn't consider pulling his ass out of that police car and beating him to death. But like you said, that would not be good for us in the long run. After all, how much of a marriage could we have if I'm in jail?"

"That would really mess up our sex life, but I would wait for you."

He laughed and pulled me close. "Thank you, but I plan to be a hands-on husband."

"Good, because that's the only kind I want."

The next day I was determined to get back to our normal routines, which included going to work.

That also meant going back to the scene to get my car.

Nicholas insisted on inspecting the vehicle and driving it around the block to make sure it hadn't been tampered with before letting me drive off to work.

I was functioning pretty well until the detective on the case called to tell me Keith had made bail. He assured me Keith had been served the restraining order so I should be safe. I prayed he was right.

It was almost time to leave work, but I didn't know if I could. I was even afraid to open the door.

My destination was Nicholas's house, not mine. I comforted myself with the knowledge that Keith didn't even know where that was, let alone have a key. There was also an alarm system, yet I was afraid to walk inside by myself.

I called Nicholas.

"Hi, what's up?" he said.

"He's out on bail."

"Is that making you nervous?"

"Yes. I know I shouldn't be but I guess I'm just a wimp."

"You're not a wimp. Do you want me to come get you?"

"Yes," I jumped at the offer. But I've gotta grow up sometime. "No, I should be able to go home by myself. I'm supposed to be getting married soon. I shouldn't need my hand held to go through a door."

"I think your apprehension is a normal reaction."

"Maybe, but I want to be back to the way things were. I'll call my parents and if they're home I'll go there and you can meet me, okay?" I asked.

"Okay, call me right back."

Yes, I did feel like a scared child afraid to walk through a door alone, but it was how I was feeling and I was grateful to have Nicholas understand and be there for me.

By the weekend, I was feeling less anxious, but apparently still a little disoriented because I agreed to go shopping with my mother and my sister.

We were all looking for dresses for the wedding. My mother vetoed most of the ones Stephanie and I liked. It was like a flashback to our teen years. Eventually I found a dress that I wanted that met with my mother's approval.

"Yes, that is acceptable, much more appropriate than the dresses you looked at before. It covers what it needs to cover. After all, this is still a church wedding," my mother said as I modeled the white tea-length dress I had chosen.

Of course my mother found a dress she liked fairly easily. Stephanie whispered, "Old lady dresses are easy to find. They make a million of them for the church crowd."

The final challenge of the day was getting Roberta and Stephanie Powell to agree on what Stephanie should wear. My sister loved colors and of course plunging necklines and splits practically up to her split.

"I'm 23, not 73! I want to look my age."

"You can look your age without showing your behind. You will be in a church, not a club! Stephanie Michelle Powell, you will not embarrass us on your sister's wedding day."

"I have to feel unencumbered in my clothes."

It took five stores and a lot of prayer, but we were able to find a dress that Stephanie would be seen in and my mother could allow her to come to church in. I only hoped my sister would not have the dress radically altered and give my mother a heart attack on my wedding day. I had already had enough drama.

I was confident I would sail seamlessly through to my wedding day.

Chapter 21

It was after 7:00 p.m. and Nicholas still wasn't home. He hadn't called to say he would be late. I tried his office and got voicemail. Same with his cell phone. That was odd, but I tried not to worry. Nicholas was just busy, I said to myself.

I had already put the food away and cleaned up the kitchen, still nothing. I texted him and stared at my phone, willing a response. I then moved to the window, hoping he was driving up.

It was easier to be mad at him than to be worried about him, so I decided Nicholas was just being thoughtless. He was one to get caught up in his work. Hadn't I been taken for granted before because of that?

I opted for a nice long bath. I popped on some music and lit the bathroom with candles. I sang along badly to the love songs for over an hour and ignored the ringing of the house phone. Finally—after all this time he was calling me back.

Nicholas had left a message that he was working late. His boss Sam had called a late meeting. I didn't call back.

When he finally came home, I was in bed reading.

"I'm sorry, baby. I meant to call before it got to be too late," Nicholas said as he kissed me.

"That's what I thought. I would not have checked the hospitals until the morning," I said without looking up from my book.

"I'm sorry and I will make it up to you."

Yes, you will, I thought.

❦

We decided to do dinner and a movie Saturday night. Since Nicholas had gone into the office for a few hours that morning, I had assumed he was all mine for the rest of the weekend.

The second time his phone rang during dinner I became slightly annoyed. I tried to let it go. We still had the movie.

I knew he had put his phone on vibrate. I had offered to keep it in my purse too, but my fiancé declined. The next time, Nicholas excused himself to take a call. When he returned, he had the nerve to bring me candy from the concession stand.

Chocolate was not going to save his butt this time.

He tried to apologize in the car. "I'm sorry, baby. Sam is really on everybody because of this merger. I promise things will calm down."

I was skeptical and a little nervous. I knew where ambition had taken Nicholas before.

Chapter 22

I busied myself with wedding preparations and the mundane as well. Nicholas was always at work. He couldn't help me screen housekeepers, so much of the cleaning and errands fell to me.

Left alone once again on another Saturday morning, I was going through Nicholas's pockets before taking some things to the cleaners. What I found made me question everything.

I had no idea what I should do. I could leave before he got home. Or I could wait for him and punch him in the eye.

Of course, good and steady Alexandra, I waited patiently.

Nicholas strolled in wearing his usual confidence so well.

"Hey, beautiful," he said and tried to kiss me.

I avoided his kiss.

"What's wrong?"

I handed him his business card where he had written on the back, 'Samantha, rm 308, Hilton'.

Nicholas smiled an innocent, guilt-free smile, "Sam is my boss, room 308 is a conference room not a hotel room."

He tried unsuccessfully once again to touch me.

"How come I'm just finding out your boss Sam is a woman?"

"Does it matter? I'm not cheating on you, Alex."

"So she's the one you've been spending all that time with on the phone and in the office?"

"Yes, once again, Sam is the boss. Look, I'm tired. I'm going to take a nap," Nicholas said then kissed the top of my head. "You want to join me?"

Chapter 23

I left him to his nap. I was angry, but about what? Did I suspect Nicholas was lying? Not really. Was I mad that he dismissed my concerns? Maybe. Was I a little afraid that he might fuel his ambition the way he had before? Maybe.

I did what I normally did when I got upset. I went shopping. It was truly therapeutic—in part because it was Nicholas's money I was spending. He might regret giving me his debit card when the statement came in. I was not feeling guilty.

Nicholas was awake when I got home. He didn't comment on my purchases. "Do you want to go out for dinner?"

"I ate at the mall," I said over my shoulder as I put the bags at the bottom of the steps.

"Are you still mad at me?"

"Perhaps."

"I have not been cheating. You have no reason not to trust me."

"I hope that's true."

"You hope?" Nicholas asked. "Alexandra, I am the best damn man you know. I have loved you forever and treated you like a queen. You cannot call that into question."

I spun around at him. "*Alexandra?*" It was all I could do to keep my hands to myself. "You have to admit that note was suspicious." I immediately wished I hadn't said that.

"Let's not forget who was engaged to somebody else when you fell into bed with me."

That hurt.

Chapter 24

This is not what I was expecting. What happened to my Prince Charming? How could he say that to me? I just looked at him in disbelief and left the room.

"I'm sorry," I heard him say as I climbed the stairs. He might have followed me if the house phone hadn't rung. He answered and then said, "It's for you."

Of course it was Stephanie. I do vaguely remember her saying she was coming over to borrow something for an event tonight.

"Yes," I said into the phone.

"I just wanted to make sure you were home, I'm on my way. You sound horrible. I'll get the details when I arrive."

I stayed upstairs until I heard the doorbell.

Stephanie was sporting a jet black ponytail with a skin tight black dress and stiletto pumps to match.

"Wow, you two look like you just found out you were first cousins. What's wrong? Did Keith show up?"

"We're fine," I lied.

Stephanie looked at Nicholas. "Nicholas, have you fucked up?"

"Alex and I are just fine. All relationships hit a little gravel from time to time."

"Okay, well it better be fine. Alex, where is the shawl I wanted? I need to be on my way. Don't make me have to make you disappear, Nicholas."

⚜

Alone again, Nicholas took my hand and led me to the sofa.

"I am sorry. I never ever want to disappoint you. You are the love of my life. Please know that my success at work is nothing if I don't have you. If you want me to step back and take a lesser job, I will."

"Thank you, Nicholas. I love you and I love that you are ambitious. I just don't want your ambition to come between us ever again. Your work has a way of consuming you." *And I remember what you did to cope last time around.*

Nicholas moved closer on the sofa. "Baby, there's nothing I want to be consumed by other than you." I felt his lips brush my cheek.

"You know I just get a little worried sometimes," I said, and let him touch me for the first time in hours. "I trust you, and I'm not asking you to downsize your career goals for your flaky fiancée."

"I don't find you flaky at all." Nicholas' hands snaked under my shirt. "I think you are just what I need."

This time when I went upstairs, Nicholas followed and we were in the mood for something other than reading.

Chapter 25

All that was left was to marry Nicholas. As the wedding approached, everything that had led us to that day was behind us. All that mattered was a new life together.

My mother had forced me to spend the night before my wedding at my parents' house, so Nicholas and I were restricted to phone contact.

"This time tomorrow we will be on our honeymoon," I told him.

"Our abbreviated honeymoon, we'll take a nice long one later on."

I looked down at the pink bedspread and smiled as I realized I would never sleep in this twin-sized bed again. "I can't wait. Can we go to Jamaica so I can meet the rest of my in-laws?"

"Maybe, but isn't the honeymoon supposed to be alone time for the newlyweds?"

"Nicholas, there is more to life than sex."

"I know, but few are more fun. I will take you to meet my family if that's what you want."

I was feeling generous. "Thank you," I said. "Maybe I'll let you have your white maid back."

"I appreciate that, but Lisa's days were probably numbered anyway. I'm sure one hot summer day when she showed up in a bikini, you would have shown her the door."

"And did she do that often?"

"All the time during the summer. Her car doesn't have air conditioning."

"Well, there goes any lingering guilt I felt about firing her."

"You had lingering guilt? It didn't sound like it when you were ordering me to get rid of her on the spot."

"I never ordered you to do anything. I merely asked."

"As I recall, I wanted to get busy and you were having none of it until I got rid of Lisa. I got the impression I was cut off until it was done."

"Oh baby, I couldn't do that. I would have been so over that by tomorrow."

"So does that mean that Alexandra Paxton does not believe in withholding the love the way Alexandra Powell does?"

"Yes, in the same way Nicholas the married man would never have some skinny white girl parading through his house in a bikini the way that Nicholas the single man did. I think that means we are a match made in heaven."

"I think so, too."

Close to midnight, my mother came in and interrupted our call. She said it was bad luck to communicate on the day of the wedding.

"Since when do you believe in superstition?" I asked.

"One word... 'Nicholas'," she said and left the room with my cell phone in hand.

Chapter 26

Okay, the day finally arrived. I was in the bridal room with Stephanie and my mom. Stephanie made sure I knew what became of Keith and his family.

Keith had agreed to a plea bargain that allowed him to get off with probation and mandatory therapy. Patricia had gone to Reverend Raymond and tried to get my family kicked out of the church. The reverend informed Patricia that our family had been members longer than hers, and had never done anything to warrant being kicked out. The Howards would have to be the ones to go.

Then Patricia hired a maid from a flier that was left on her door. The cute blonde was a big hit with Bill, her husband—so much so that one day Patricia came home early to find the maid polishing Bill instead of the silver. The couple is now embroiled in a nasty divorce.

I was being escorted down the aisle on the arm of my father. Waiting for me was my love, Nicholas. Was my confident man just a little bit nervous? Maybe, but he certainly looked fine in that black suit, tailor made for his body. I had to remind myself that we were in church and suppress certain thoughts.

We promised to love, honor, and cherish each other and be each other's best friend; and then we got to hear the words we had been waiting for.

"I now pronounce you husband and wife. You may kiss the bride."

Before we were able to skip town and enjoy our honeymoon weekend, we had a reception of sorts in a restaurant. Since we only had our immediate families, the crowd fit at one table. It was our first gathering all together and everybody seemed to enjoy themselves. Some more than others—as Stephanie was checking out Nicholas's best man, Chris, who was the guy he was having lunch with when we had met again a few months ago.

By evening time, we were in our hotel suite at the Plaza in New York City and celebrating our marriage... over and over again. New York was special because it's where Nicholas and I had made love for the first time, and now where we made love for the first time as husband and wife. Of course, Nicholas's checkbook as a business executive was a lot heftier than as a college student, so no more Holiday Inns. The Plaza was a five-star hotel for sure. They even cleaned your room twice a day if you desired. That would not be necessary this weekend.

I could not have been more content wrapped in my husband's arms wearing nothing but the rings he slipped on my finger. I was in love and that's exactly where I planned to stay for the rest of my life.

About the Author

Valerie Landrum retired from federal government to focus on writing and volunteering. She lives in York County, Pennsylvania.

www.ingramcontent.com/pod-product-compliance
Lightning Source LLC
Chambersburg PA
CBHW070604180626
46817CB00005B/1995